# Roland Argan

## The legendary assassin who killed the demon lord

A brilliant assassin who single-handedly killed the demon lord extolled for being the most powerful ever. The official story is that he and the demon lord both died in battle. Roland became regarded as a legendary figure who ended the war between humans and demons.

# Rileyla Diakitep

## The most powerful former demon lord of all time

The former demon lord and Roland's current demonic lover. Nicknamed Rila. She's taken a liking to Roland, who defeated her by himself. Now she acts as Roland's familiar and lives with him.

## Iris Negan

### The cool guild branch manager

An icy woman, she is infamous for being strict with herself and others. As the person who interviews and recruits Roland, she is one of the few who know his true identity, other than the guild head.

## Almelia Felind

### The naive former hero

A hero and the first princess of the Felind Kingdom. Originally, she was on a journey to slay the demon lord with Roland. After the demon lord's assassination, her duty was fulfilled, and she returned to her homeland.

## Milia McGuffin

### The bright associate guild colleague

A guild receptionist. As the newest guild employee prior to Roland joining, she acts as his mentor. She quickly takes a liking to her first-ever mentee and becomes a little too helpful.

THE GUILD MEMBER WITH A WORTHLESS SKILL IS ACTUALLY A LEGENDARY ASSASSIN

"What an entertaining guest I have."

Just like that, the assassin who defeated the so-called most powerful demon lord had become a legend. Without anyone knowing...

"If you've got any last words, let's hear them."

# HAZURE SKILL

## THE GUILD MEMBER WITH A WORTHLESS SKILL IS ACTUALLY A LEGENDARY ASSASSIN

**Kennoji**

ILLUSTRATION BY
**KWKM**

YEN ON

New York

Hazure Skill: The Guild Member with a Worthless Skill Is Actually a Legendary Assassin, Vol. 1
Kennoji

Translation by Jan Mitsuko Cash
Cover art by KWKM

HAZURE SKILL "KAGE GA USUI" WO MOTSU GUILD SHOKUIN GA,
JITSU WA DENSETSU NO ANSATSUSHA Vol. 1
©Kennoji, KWKM 2019
First published in Japan in 2019 by KADOKAWA CORPORATION, Tokyo.
English translation rights arranged with KADOKAWA CORPORATION, Tokyo
through TUTTLE-MORI AGENCY, INC., Tokyo.

Yen On
150 West 30th Street, 19th Floor
New York, NY 10001

Visit us at yenpress.com
facebook.com/yenpress
twitter.com/yenpress
yenpress.tumblr.com
instagram.com/yenpress

First Yen On Edition: April 2021

Yen On is an imprint of Yen Press, LLC.
The Yen On name and logo are trademarks of Yen Press, LLC.

The publisher is not responsible for websites (or their content) that are not owned by the publisher.

Library of Congress Cataloging-in-Publication Data
Names: Kennoji, author. | KWKM, illustrator. | Cash, Jan Mitsuko, translator.
Title: Hazure skill, the guild member with a worthless skill is actually a legendary
     assassin / Kennoji ; illustration by KWKM ; translation by Jan Mitsuko Cash.
Other titles: Hazure sukiru kage ga usui o motsu girudo shokuin ga jitsu wa
     densetsu no ansatsusha. English
Description: First Yen On edition. | New York : Yen On, 2021.
Identifiers: LCCN 2020055761 | ISBN 9781975318772 (v. 1 ; trade paperback)
Subjects: LCSH: Assassins—Fiction. | GSAFD: Fantasy.
Classification: LCC PL872.5.K46 H3913 2021 | DDC 895.63/6—dc23
LC record available at https://lccn.loc.gov/2020055761

ISBNs: 978-1-9753-1877-2 (paperback)
       978-1-9753-1878-9 (ebook)

10 9 8 7 6 5 4 3 2 1

LSC-C

Printed in the United States of America

# HAZURE SKILL

## THE GUILD MEMBER WITH A WORTHLESS SKILL IS ACTUALLY A LEGENDARY ASSASSIN

# CONTENTS

# 1

# The Last Mission

"All right, this plan is the best shot we have if we're going to make the most of Roland's skills!" A smile bloomed on the hero Almelia's face as she concluded her explanation.

Our party had already infiltrated the demon lord's castle and was having a last-minute strategy meeting in an empty storehouse. We were incredibly close to the audience chamber, where we would presumably find the demon lord.

To put it simply, our strategy was to have the hero, mage, high cleric, and paladin—basically everyone I'd been traveling with—distract the demon lord. Then I'd use my Unobtrusive skill's special ability to kill our enemy.

That's all there was to it.

"Almelia, isn't that supposed to be *your* job?"

It did seem strange for the hero to step out of the spotlight.

"It's fine. Besides, this plan has the highest chance of success."

Everyone else agreed.

It wasn't like *I'd* be any good at drawing the demon lord's attention—that was for sure...

"Looking at it objectively, you've got the best chance of getting it done, Roland."

When it came to our individual abilities, that was definitely true. The reasoning behind the plan was solid…

Our party had exhausted every reserve of physical strength and magic just to reach this place. Likely because of how drained we all were, there was a sense of grim resolve hanging in the air.

At this rate, somebody was going to end up dead.

No matter what lay ahead, however, these were people I'd traveled with for a long time. I wanted to see this journey through to the end without losing a single one of them.

Even though we normally got pretty talkative the moment we had a chance to rest, right now nobody had much to say. The others might've been brooding, or maybe they were quietly preparing themselves for what was coming.

I decided to excuse myself. I activated my Unobtrusive skill and tried to leave the storehouse in which we'd hidden ourselves.

"Roland, where are you going?"

Almelia easily caught me. Everyone else noticed the moment she pointed me out.

All my Unobtrusive skill did was make me more forgettable and blend into the background. It wasn't like it made me invisible, nor did it erase all traces of my presence.

In this world where everyone got a skill, mine was the letdown of all letdowns—literally the most disappointing skill.

"I'm taking a breather."

"Taking a breather…to do what?"

"To take a leak—want to come with?"

"H-honestly! Just get it done quickly! I can't believe you're not even slightly nervous at a time like this."

The party of heroes was made up of women at a tender age. I had no clue what kind of idea had gotten into Almelia's head, but her face turned red, and she shooed me away with her hand.

"I'll be back real soon."

I left the storehouse only after making sure that no enemies were around. The truth was, I didn't plan on returning to the party. In fact, I expected never to see any of them again. I was going to finish this journey without losing a single one of them.

That was my mission.

Facing the demon lord as we were ensured someone would perish.

"...All right, time to get to work."

The top floor of the demon lord's castle was eerily quiet. At the end of the long, extensive hallway, I found a monolithic and outrageously gaudy door.

...This was it.

Instead of heading that way, I climbed out one of the windows in the corridor. I leaped onto a terrace about two floors down, landing quietly.

I spotted a demon knight who'd been stationed as a guard. I drew the dagger at my hip. After covering the demon knight's mouth with my hand, I slit the creature's throat. Once it had died, I laid its limp carcass on the floor.

My companions had believed that the audience chamber where the demon lord waited could be reached only through the front entrance.

When I checked the blueprints we'd gotten our hands on, however, I found an alternate route that I could take. After showing everyone the map, I'd told them that I'd be able to get in that way.

*"There's no freaking way we could pull off the acrobatics needed to go that route,"* Almelia had said.

*"Yes, I agree,"* Elvie the paladin had added. She just didn't like heights.

*"…Looks fun…,"* Lina the mage had commented. That girl had absolutely zero reflexes to speak of, so her willingness to try was concerning.

*"Ha-ha, ha-ha. Never expected to fall to my death after coming so close to fighting the demon lord, ha-ha. This is like some sort of joke."* Serafin the high cleric had been battling a fit of laughter.

…And that's the conversation we'd had in that strategy session earlier.

I hurled up a length of rope, aiming for a spire above, and silently climbed from shadow to shadow.

Facing enemies directly was for heroes. I was going to take that demon lord *directly* by surprise instead.

Still gripping the rope, I ran along the spire wall and used my momentum to make a long leap. I reached the window of the demon lord's audience chambers—an entry point that was supposed to be absolutely impossible to infiltrate.

I inhaled sharply, then let out a slow exhale. Gathering magic in my pointer finger, I thrust it at the window. As I broke through a single point on the firm magical barrier, I simultaneously cut a hole in the glass. Attacking a specific location on the front of a defensive barrier could be quite effective.

Reaching through the hole I'd cut, I unlocked the window, raised it, and quietly slid in.

Now I was right behind the throne.

"What an entertaining guest I have."

Apparently, you couldn't pull a fast one on a demon lord. My visit had been immediately detected.

Emitting some sinister mana, the demon lord stood from the throne. We stared each other down. Before me was a figure wearing a gaudy mantle. Slitted reptilian eyes stared into mine. The demon lord's long hair was as red as fire, and her irises were a deep crimson shade.

She was beautiful, that demonic woman.

We didn't bother with chitchat.

I activated my skill—immediately using my full power to end this quickly. At the same time, the demon lord fired off magic that looked like black lightning. Despite being unfamiliar with that kind of spell, I had no trouble evading it.

That was because her attack had been directed at the wrong place.

"Hmm...?"

The demon lord realized something was off.

She sure was powerful. Even if it'd missed, her attack broke through the magical barrier placed on the room and blew out the wall with a thunderous roar. I would've been lucky to be a pile of dust if I'd taken an attack like that.

The demon lord loosed another one of those dark bolts, this time at a completely different trajectory. Much like the first one, however, it missed the mark.

"—Again...!"

I'd been turning my Unobtrusive skill on and off since we started. Skills weren't normally capable of being activated and deactivated like that, but I could use mine as if I were flipping the lights. Even though it'd appear like I was right before my opponent's eyes, I'd seem to disappear the very next instant. In reality, I was actually still right in front of the demon lord. Rapidly alternating between those states confused my opponents. The more desperate they were to find me, the worse of a situation they'd dig themselves into.

I hadn't moved a single step. Anyone confounded this much would naturally start to attack blindly.

"You little sneak…!"

The demon lord was growing irritated. Her mana, magical skills, magic sensibilities, and battle prowess were all undoubtedly exemplary.

However…

"…Demon Lord, when was the last time you actually fought anyone?"

Lords weren't commonly drawn into the fighting. I'd never even heard of this woman showing her face on the front lines. Against an opponent like me—someone who'd fought against enemies on the regular and had honed his senses—downtime was as good as fatal.

Then again, the skill I had, Unobtrusive, was a loser skill that denied me the chance of ever being a hero. To put things in a somewhat different way, however, no one used loser skills. That meant no one knew how to counter them.

Every ability had its uses…

You just had to get creative.

Understanding that was the key to making any loser skill a special one that nobody could emulate.

"First time seeing a skill like mine, huh?"

After hearing my voice, the demon lord flipped around and attacked me with a shadowy longsword that she'd fortified using her mana. By the time she swiped, I'd already turned my skill on and was long gone.

"Tsk, where are—?"

"…Right in front of you."

The moment she faced forward, I thrust a dagger at her forehead. Costing only seventeen hundred rins, my weapon was pretty cheap. Even a kid could've bought one of these knives if they saved up their allowance for a bit.

I didn't need any special gear or the like. Even a weapon was just a tool in the end. *I'm* my greatest weapon. That idea had been driven into me countless times during my tenure as an assassin.

"Guh… I shall acknowledge my defeat… I shall scale down the demon lord army and thereafter dissolve it. I will instruct my forces not to harm any humans as they retreat."

The demon lord fell to her knees.

"That's not even on the table for discussion."

Even if she actually did dissolve her army and forbade them from harming humans, the possibility for war would remain so long as the demon lord's banner flew.

Protecting the party of heroes and assassinating the demon lord—those were my duties.

Abandoning them now wasn't an option.

"If you've got any last words, let's hear them."

At my command, the demon lord raised her bowed head. She looked relieved. It was almost as though a huge burden had finally been lifted from her. Perhaps she'd been prepared for this.

I then killed the demon lord.

With that, my mission was complete.

I walked out the front door alone and put the demon lord's castle behind me.

Just like that, the assassin who defeated the so-called most powerful demon lord had become a legend. Without anyone knowing...

# 2
# Report at the Royal Castle

"…And so the demon lord is gone."

I was in the king's private chambers. After defeating the demon lord, I'd reported the good news to King Randolf, the man who'd hired me for the task.

"Oh! Ohhh…! You did an excellent job!"

A tad over forty, King Randolf was a good-natured man who I'd describe as neither overbearing nor foolish.

"I never would've guessed that the strongest, and quite possibly most sinister, demon lord in history would be so easily…"

"The report may have made it sound easy, but had Almelia and the others not been there, I never would've even been able to step foot in the castle."

While I was probably the strongest in the party when it came to one-on-one fights, Almelia the hero and Lina the mage were more powerful against multiple opponents. My ability just didn't have the kind of firepower necessary for large groups. Serafin the high cleric was an unexpectedly good problem solver, and Elvie the paladin protected everyone, her strong sense of justice often helping us make the right decisions. With everyone's unique qualities combined, I thought we made a good team.

"Even if I was the one who asked it of you, I still find it hard to believe that you defeated the demon lord on your own…"

"An assassin's specialty lies in one-on-one battles. That's all there is to it."

I couldn't speak for other assassins, but my elimination techniques didn't assume taking on multiple enemies. That was how I'd been taught, and that was the sort of combat style to which I'd devoted myself. Heroes, mages, and the other classes would build up their training with the assumption that they'd face all kinds of situations, but that wasn't the way of the assassin. We'd wait for particular circumstances, or even create them, and aim for the opportunity to make a guaranteed kill.

That's what assassination work was.

"Did you use some kind of special skill?" asked the king.

"Not particularly," I replied.

All I could use was Unobtrusive. Naturally, I couldn't call something like that "special." Actually, it was considered to be one of the washout skills. I could use some magic, but a capability in that regard would've amounted to child's play when facing a demon lord.

Apparently, it was generally accepted that direct abilities used for attack, defense, healing, or boosting were the winners. I'd heard that from all over while I was with the party. Sure, if an ordinary person used my skill, it'd be a big flop. All they'd accomplish would be keeping others from noticing them for a fleeting moment. It didn't truly make you invisible, after all. Supported by my assassination techniques, physical prowess, and battle experience, however, that loser skill of mine took on a different light.

Ever since I realized that Unobtrusive held a kind of useful synergy with assassination, I'd been hard at work every day trying to devise new ways to capitalize on that.

"I suppose the assassination of the demon lord could be called the culmination of your career."

"It's not nearly that dramatic. I just…needed to do it in order to live."

"By the gods, you're a modest man."

"It's the truth."

"Well, I've received personal reports from Almelia and the others. According to them, things weren't going well before you joined. Their battle capabilities and cooperation seem to have climbed rapidly since you got involved."

"They give me too much credit."

"Nonsense. You slew the demon lord—a feat said to have been impossible. And you did it single-handedly, no less. It wasn't just Almelia—Elvie, Lina, and Serafin all said the same thing of you. They told me they never would've reached the demon lord's castle without you, Roland."

"It's give and take… The same could be said for any of them."

"You really won't admit what a triumph you've accomplished, will you? Your victory over the demon lord will make you a living legend."

"Please, that's quite enough. Such renown is too heavy a burden to bear. It doesn't suit me. I'd much rather remain in obscurity."

"Well, all right, but you will allow me to prepare a banquet for you. You may spend some time in the castle at your leisure."

"I'll have to politely decline. In the end, it was the hero Almelia and the others who defeated the demon lord… Isn't that right?"

The world's light was too blinding for a person of the shadows like me.

"That certainly aligns with the request I made of you…"

King Randolf's appeal had been for me to support the party of heroes and assassinate the demon lord. However, he'd also asked that the heroes get credit for the victory.

"The hero Almelia Felind is also the Felind Kingdom's first princess. Her pedigree and talents make her the ideal candidate to be made a legend. As a proud father, surely you agree?"

"You forgot to mention that she's intelligent and beautiful as well, Roland."

*He's right*, I thought as I gave a forced smile at King Randolf's coddling remark.

It was true that Almelia was intelligent and beautiful. I'd thought that the reason the king had asked me to kill the demon lord and protect Almelia and the others had been to maintain the Felind Kingdom's image of strength and political influence over other nations. In actuality, he might've simply been concerned about his daughter.

"Still, sending home a legendary assassin empty-handed would be a disgrace to the Felind royal family, Roland. Is there nothing you desire? I can give you damsels of beauty beyond compare. If you'd prefer money, name any sum you like. If you wish for a house, I will prepare one posthaste."

"What I desire…"

I didn't have many childhood memories. I'd just been raised by my assassin master in place of parents. Most of my formative years had been spent honing my skills. I didn't even know my real name. In all honestly, I had no idea what to request.

"If you asked me how to kill someone, I'd be able to tell you right away, but I have no idea what I myself desire."

Up until that point, I'd been occupied with killing various people and monsters.

"Oh!" King Randolf exclaimed, giving me pause. "I said I'd let you have beautiful damsels, but you can't have Almelia. Not her. She's just sixteen. She's not old enough to become a bride!"

Arranging an engagement between a sixteen-year-old princess and the prince of some foreign land didn't seem all that odd to me, but apparently, the king had no plans to marry off his daughter so easily. Even if he didn't give her up, though, there were likely to be as many suitors for her hand as there were stars in the sky.

"Harrumph." King Randolf crossed his arms as he grumbled. "How…however, Roland…if you were to say you want Almelia's hand in marriage…! I, Randolf, would cry tears of my very own blood, but I'd let her—"

"No thanks. I don't need her."

"You don't?!"

*Ahhh, good.* King Randolf seemed genuinely relieved. He really was a pretty likable king.

"However, it's a bit disappointing in its own way to hear that you don't want her…"

Apparently, this proud father just couldn't accept that I'd declined the hand of Almelia.

Bringing up the princess brought something to mind. Back during some point of our journey, Almelia had said she wanted to try "*living a normal life.*" We'd wondered about what "*normal*" actually was, but none of us knew. No one in our party had ever experienced such a thing. The only lifestyles I'd ever known were living deep in the mountains with my master during training and my days working as an assassin.

I doubted any of that was normal.

"…A normal life."

"Hmm? What about it?" asked the king.

"I'd like to try living what you'd call a 'normal life.' Instead of living as an assassin, I'd like a plain, mundane life. The kind an average person would lead."

In such a position, I could earn money without having to kill people or monsters. I could be at peace without deceiving anyone. I wouldn't have to worry about betrayals.

"Are you sure that's all you want? Being surrounded by a crowd of beautiful women and spending your days cavorting with them isn't a bad life, either."

"Don't lump me in with the likes of you, King Randolf."

"What are you saying? Begetting children is a legitimate part of my work," King Randolf replied indignantly, though jokingly so. "Do as you like, I suppose. I believe I understand why *normal* is relatively difficult to obtain. In addition to allotting you your new, average life, I will provide anything else you may require."

The original reward was that he would fulfill any desires I had.

"I imagine you'll need something to cover living expenses," the king declared, giving me a sum of about a million rins. "Is that enough?" he asked, seeming uneasy.

"It's plenty, and I'm sure it'll be a great help. Thank you," I replied.

"What are you saying? I'm the one who should be thanking *you*."

King Randolf and I exchanged a firm handshake.

*Scritch-scratch. Scritch-scratch-scritch.* A scraping sound could be heard outside, and a black cat entered through a crack in the door.

"A cat...? Did a stray wander in...? No, it seems to have a collar," muttered the king.

*Meow.* The black cat gave a cry. I patted its head and scratched its neck when it came up to my feet.

"Roland, if you should find that there's anything else you need—"

I shook my head and cut King Randolf off before he could finish. "This is enough. It's your job to make the world into a place where my services aren't required."

The king gave me a strained smile. "That it is. Then let us pray we never meet again. Especially not as enemies."

"That should be fine. I don't think *normal people* regularly have audiences with kings."

After saying that, I left the king's chambers behind me. The black cat followed.

*Meow, meow,* it cried and started to scratch at its collar with its hind leg.

"All right, I get it."

The collar was a kind of magical equipment. It was a pretty rare item, but I was glad I'd had it on me.

After I touched the collar and routed some magic through it, the cat faintly glowed and transformed into a human shape.

"That feline form really doesn't suit me; I cannot help it."

She brushed away the red hair that had come to rest on her

shoulder. Her name was Rileyla Diakitep. Since her actual name was long, she'd told me to call her Rila.

"I imagine you'll get used to that soon enough."

"I couldn't help but overhear that the legendary man who defeated *me, the demon lord,* desired a *normal life…* What a strange man you are."

Rila laughed.

"Look who's talking! You're the piddling demon lord who couldn't even put up a fight against that strange man for ten minutes."

In addition to shape-shifting, the collar sapped strength from the wearer in proportion to how much mana they possessed. The specialized item, which could even be called Rila's worst nightmare, was something I'd brought with me to counter her. Selling it would've no doubt earned me enough to build my own castle.

Back when the demon lord had "died," we'd left a fake corpse of Rila's making in that audience chamber. Once that was done, I'd departed the demon lord's castle.

"*I crafted this masterpiece by gathering the essence of my magical arts. Even the upper echelons of my demonic army won't be able to see through such a ruse. And that's assuming they've survived!*"

Rila had been fully confident.

When it came to the humans, I was the only one who'd ever seen the demon lord up close.

After defeating Rila, I'd put a collar on her that she could never take off. In that moment, the being known as the demon lord had died, in a manner of speaking.

"You are an unexpectedly charitable man."

"The only reason I let you live was because I didn't have any other way to use the collar. Even if I sold it, there's a chance it'd be misused. Plus, I wouldn't have any use for the money I'd get for it."

Even though I'd left Rila to live as a cat for the rest of her days, she'd followed me anyway.

"Regardless of how it may appear, I *am* grateful you relieved me of the responsibility of being the demon lord." As Rila spoke in a singsong voice, she entangled her hand in mine. For some unfathomable reason, she'd apparently taken a liking to me. "Really now, you're an assassin, and you failed to get the job done. Ha-ha-ha-ha."

"Yeah, that's right. That's why I'm retiring from assassin work starting today," I replied.

"So where are you off to now?" Rila looked gleeful as she latched onto my elbow.

Since that made it hard to walk, I tried brushing her off, but her arms were like a vise, and she refused to let go. Despite having lost her mana, it seemed she still had the strength of a normal woman.

"That's obvious. I'm heading to a place that's neither urban nor rural—I'm going to a *normal town*."

"Oh, that *normal* rubbish again… The prospect scarcely sounds thrilling to me at all…"

"I'm not doing this for you."

Rila flashed me a pout as we disappeared into the royal capital's crowds.

# 3
# The Interview

"I wonder what a *normal life* is supposed to be like?"

An average town… It took me about two weeks to get to Lahti, a settlement that fit my requirements of neither being too much like a city or too much like the countryside. Since we didn't have a house, Rila and I chose a cheap inn to stay at.

It was a little before lunchtime but still after breakfast.

"Do you think I know what a normal *human* life is?" Rila asked as she clung to me naked in bed. "We spend every day like this, eating and having sex in turn… That isn't bad in its own way, but…even I, a demon lord, know that such a thing isn't a *normal life*."

"Still, I think it's a *normal activity* for most people."

I ate and slept, then went to sleep with her. It wasn't hard to imagine that'd be *normal* for a man to do. The first time we did the deed, I'd asked Rila if she was sure.

*"I've already decided. I want to offer everything to the man who was more powerful than I was. What's more, you're a good person."*

Her motives almost seemed far-fetched. I just really didn't understand demonkind's values.

Perhaps listening to my heartbeat, she put her head on my chest.

"So this is how humans and demons proliferate... I can see why people do this over and over again..."

Rila turned away from me. Her shoulders were slender, and her back was white. For an overwhelmingly powerful demon lord, she looked no different than a fifteen- or sixteen-year-old girl in this state.

"You can see? See what, exactly?" I asked.

"Sex... It...feels good...," she said in a whisper like the buzz of a mosquito.

Even though she'd been a virgin until just a little while ago, it seemed she'd really taken a liking to this.

"Your ears are beet red... Are you all right?"

"Oh."

Rila yanked the blanket and made for an escape beneath the covers.

*Klunk-klunk.* Right at that moment, I heard a knock at the door.

I immediately touched Rila's collar and turned her into a cat.

"Um? Mr. Argan? Are you in?"

*Argan...* For a second, I wondered who that was; then I recalled it was the surname I'd assumed. Perhaps it was because I'd changed my identity so often, but I was having trouble answering to the last name I'd randomly chosen.

"I've come to retrieve tonight's lodging fees."

"Okay, sure. I'll be right there—"

I quickly put on my clothes and opened the door.

The daughter of the innkeeper stood in the hall.

I paid the fees for the upcoming week in one lump sum.

"Thank you very much. And, ummm... There is a slight issue... Um, uh, we've heard rather *passionate* noises every night... And not just at night but sometimes in the afternoon and morning..."

When I thought back on it, Rila and I had indulged in our carnal desires regardless of the time of day or night.

*Mrow.* A black cat passed by my feet and left the room.

"Huh...? A kitty?" the innkeeper's daughter asked.

"Those noises might've been her meowing."

It wasn't entirely inaccurate.

"Oh, what have I done? I can't believe I made such an embarrassing mistake— I-I'm so sorry."

The girl bobbed in a bow.

I smiled gently as if to say, *Not at all*, and shook my head.

"Mr. Argan, what is it that you do?"

*Hmm, what do I do?*

"I eat, sleep, and have sex."

"Huh?"

*Was that not what she wanted to know...?* I was sure I'd answered the exact thing I'd been asked.

"No! Th-that wasn't what I meant. I meant for work! What do you do for work? Are you a traveler?"

"Oh, right... Work..."

One of the things *normal* men did was work. All I knew was the art of assassination, but regular people did something more akin to the art of earning a living. Truthfully, if I kept spending at the rate I was, I was likely to bottom out pretty soon. King Randolf would probably give me more money if I asked, but that definitely wasn't *normal*.

"Actually, I'm looking for work...," I decided.

"I thought so! In that case, why don't you become an adventurer? I hear that the exam isn't difficult, and if you're successful, it's a way to get rich fast."

"I'm not sure about that kind of work... I'm not particularly strong..."

I'd seen the escorts of my assassination targets and knew that adventurers didn't lead *normal lives*. Truthfully, that sort of occupation could get fairly extreme.

The innkeeper's daughter looked me up and down, then nodded in agreement. "You certainly are thin and slender, Mr. Argan. You'd probably have a hard time with physical labor..."

For assassins, the way we carried ourselves, our flexibility, and our dynamism were key. That's why we eschewed any unnecessary muscle.

"Oh! In that case, why don't you become an employee at the Adventurers Guild? When I walked by the guild building earlier, I saw a recruitment flyer. I don't think there's much physical work involved, either."

"That's it...!"

A job like that would allow me to make use of the experiences I'd gained traveling with Almelia and the others. I had knowledge about battling. Giving advice to amateurs was sure to be easy. It was the perfect opportunity, and I wanted to seize upon it before it was too late.

Thanking the young woman, I immediately got ready to head

out. My sights were set on the Adventurers Guild. Thankfully, I'd learned my way around town during my short stay, so I found the place rather easily.

"Welcome to the Adventurers Guild. Will it be a quest today? Or do you need to register as an adventurer?"

"No, I came to see the recruitment flyer."

"Oh, are you applying? Branch Managerrrrr? We have an applicant!" The receptionist flipped around and called for her superior.

A long-haired woman poked her face out from the back of the room. Our eyes met.

"We'll conduct the interview here." She ushered me toward her with a hand.

The receptionist smiled and offered a few encouraging words. "Don't worry—the interview is nothing unusual. Good luck anyway, though!"

*A normal* interview… *I see.* As someone aiming to be utterly average, it couldn't have been more perfect. I needed to put some oomph into this. I walked to the room I'd been instructed to go to and knocked on the door.

"Please come in."

Entering, I sat myself down on a nearby sofa.

The woman who'd been referred to as "*Branch Manager*" just a few moments before introduced herself as Iris Negan. Her most notable feature was undoubtedly her stern eyes. As far as looks went, she was a slim, beautiful woman in her mid-twenties. She stood around five feet, four inches tall.

I introduced myself as well. "I'm Roland Argan, twenty-five. It's a pleasure to meet you."

The age I'd given was chosen at random. According to the members of the party of heroes, I apparently looked to be anywhere from my teens to my thirties. I didn't know my own age, so I regularly changed it on the spot. It was likely that I was indeed around twenty-five years old, so that was what I told most people, unless there was a reason to lie.

The branch manager, Iris, asked me several questions, and I answered them all in kind.

"Do you have adventurer experience?"

The answer was naturally no.

"Any skills?"

Unwilling to share details on that matter with someone I'd just met, I instead made something up.

"Do you have any operational experience working in other guilds, even if it wasn't an Adventurers Guild?"

That was also a no.

Iris the branch manager gave an exasperated sigh.

"Listen up. We might be recruiting, but that doesn't mean we'll hire just anyone. Types like you are a dime a dozen, not to mention nuisances. Too many people underestimate guild work."

"That's not my intention at all."

It didn't seem like Iris would believe me if I told her that I'd defeated a demon lord. Even if she did, that'd be the end of my *normal* life where no one paid attention to me, so I didn't volunteer any of that information.

This was a problem.

Even if I kept my history under wraps, only saying that I'd gone on some adventures and knew a thing or two about monsters, I got the feeling Iris wouldn't accept it.

"Well, it's all right. Our guild doesn't care who you are or where you're from. What's important is that you excel at something—anything. I wouldn't mind giving you the gig if you've got some kind of talent you can provide."

If that was really the case, then this job was in the bag.

Iris the branch manager had just said that having a talent was much more important than those earlier questions.

"Just to be sure, what do you mean by something I excel at?" I asked.

"For example, a former adventurer might specialize in swordsmanship. That's just one possibility, though; it could be anything. A knowledge of magic, a thorough understanding of items, an expertise with plants, animal handling, monster biology—"

I flicked a pebble with my thumb so that it made a high-pitched clinking sound against the windowpane. Iris turned to look at the source of the disturbance, and I took that opportunity to turn on my skill. Apparently, opening up to Iris about my unusual ability was my way into employment.

"...Huh? Well anyway, adventurers take quests, and you'll need to deal with them at the reception window. There are times when you might have to fight, though. You look like you're a bit of a softy; do you really think you'll be all right?"

"I don't know too much about what adventurers are like, but... when it comes to excelling at a certain talent, I believe I'm a good fit," I assured her.

"Hmph," Iris snorted. "You sure sound confident. Don't tell me your amazing ability is just that you're a little flexible or quick to get dressed, is it? If it's something that anyone could accomplish, it doesn't count."

"Do you know what this is?"

I showed Iris a piece of cloth. It was black in color, triangular, and the whole thing was warm from residual body heat.

"Hmm? Is that women's underwear...? Ah! I-is that mine?! D-did you...?! Did you steal my underwear from my hous—?"

I raised a hand to stop Iris's irate inquiry. "I *did* steal them, but I have no idea where you live... Have you really not noticed yet?"

Iris looked down, checking for something.

Her face had already been red, but the color deepened even further.

"Ah! Wh-when did you...?! You took them off me...?! I know— it was magic! That's some kind of specialized skill!"

"You took your eyes off me the moment you heard something, right? That's when I did it," I said.

We were right next to each other in a space less than ten feet apart. Iris had turned to glance at the window after hearing that sound I made. Even such a brief moment was more than enough time to do my work.

By making free use of my Unobtrusive skill, I could take off her underwear or do anything else I wanted. Having deft fingers was a necessary part of such a feat, too, however.

This was the first time I'd ever used my skill to pull off someone's undergarments.

In order to make the target unaware of my presence using Unobtrusive, I needed to hide any indication of myself, take steps without making a sound, and move at high speeds in a very brief amount of time. I had learned all of these during my time as an assassin. I was first-rate at acting swiftly without leaving any indication I had been there. This included audible footsteps and even the breeze from my movements.

Distracting someone's gaze like I had earlier was yet another technique in the assassin toolbox.

Despite being a pro and having some amount of pride for being one, it came as a surprise that Iris had forced me into using my skill…

She was tough.

*Wasn't this supposed to be a* normal *interview?*

"No way. You…did that in just a second? That's unbelievable… I didn't even notice you taking them off."

That much was to be expected. The enemies I killed often never had the chance to realize they were dead.

"Miss Iris… It seems you severely underestimated my talent."

Whether with embarrassment or anger, Iris the branch manager shook as her face flushed again.

Once more, I invoked my skill, making sure to put the underwear back where I'd found them.

"…Huh? No way! Now you've put them back on me…?!"

What else could I have done? Iris was stuck staring down at her desk while trembling slightly. She was overcome with embarrassment and anger. Her panties were a secondary or even a tertiary concern to her. While she was in such a state, redressing her was a piece of cake.

"…Then that means you saw my private bits? Twice?!"

Iris pursed her lips as her face seemed to steam and flood with red.

"…F-fine, I'll admit you have talent…"

"Huh? Um, you were speaking so quietly, I couldn't hear you."

"I admit it! I acknowledge your ability! I might even allow you to work for us!"

"...You might *allow* me to?"

"I want to hire you! Come work for us! I won't have you work anywhere else! I won't stand for you working anywhere other than here!"

"Thank you very much. I'll come by tomorrow, then—as a guild employee."

*So, this is a* normal interview...

Apparently, even I could get through one when I set my mind to it.

More self-assured that I'd taken a few steps toward *normalcy*, I left the office behind.

# 4

# The Former Assassin's New Job After a Career Change

"Where are you going today, knave?" asked a black cat while I was getting dressed that morning. It seemed Rila had gotten used to her feline form, even having learned how to speak while transformed.

"To work…at a regular job."

"Quite the smug look you've got there."

After noticing that a lot of the guild employees were wearing glasses, I'd picked up a lensless pair on my way back from the interview yesterday. With that, I'd succeeded in becoming even more *normal*.

"My, you do seem motivated to work despite the low wage."

Rila slid me a piece of paper using her front paws. The standard guild-employee salary was written on it. All told, it came to a hundred and fifty thousand rins. So long as I didn't live extravagantly, or rather, so long as I lived a *normal life*, I would get by. That's not to say I'd end up with a whole lot of extra money to throw around, though.

"Knave, if you were to snuff out one or two lives, you'd be able to enjoy yourself for three entire months."

"Rila, that's not a *normal* job."

"That is a *very* smug look."

"Make sure you behave."

"I couldn't make a commotion in this form even if I wished to. If you could at least return me to my original body..."

"Even if no one knows you're the demon lord, having a demonic woman hanging around wouldn't be *normal*."

"So you've learned to speak of what is *normal*, even though you don't know what that is yourself."

"See you later." I closed the door behind me and left the inn.

It was only a ten-minute walk to the Adventurers Guild. Upon arrival, I was met by the same receptionist who'd cheered me on the other day.

"Oh, is that you, Mr. Roland? I heard about you starting today from the branch manager. I'm looking forward to working with you."

Apparently, this girl had been tasked with showing me the ropes.

"I'm Milia McGuffin. Honestly, I'm still pretty impressed you were hired."

"Huh? I thought that was a *normal* interview, though?"

"No, no, you're being too modest. The branch manager Iris hasn't ever hired anyone."

*I see.* Supposedly, Milia and the other employees had been hired before Iris had become branch manager.

"I'm pretty interested in knowing more about the man who the branch manager hired on the spot..."

"It's nothing so special. I just had a normal interview with her."

"I used to be the bottom rung here, but it looks like I'll be guiding you as you get used to things. So if there's anything you're having trouble with, feel free to ask me about it. Okay, mentee? ♪"

"I will, mentor."

Clearly in a good mood after our introduction, Milia started showing me around the cramped office. Receptionists waited at counters to help any adventurers who came in, while other employees behind them sat at desks poring over documents. There were even more people in another room appraising various goods that had been brought to the office. In short, all kinds of things went on at the guild.

"So this is *normal* work…"

*I can make a living without killing anyone… What a strange world.*

Since I didn't have a clear understanding of what an adventurer was, Milia gave me a thorough explanation. Apparently, those who had registered at the guild were called adventurers. They would tackle various client orders, called quests. Sometimes they'd also go mining for rare materials or delve into dungeons to treasure hunt.

"So they're not pros or anything? Aren't they basically just amateur odd-job workers?" I inquired.

Flustered, Milia brought a finger to her lips and shushed me. "Mr. Roland, you can't say that out loud."

The Adventurers Guild acted as the go-between for those odd-job adventurers and the clients. Part of our responsibility was to determine a quest's difficulty and pick out the right people for it.

"Look," Milia called. "Someone's just finished a quest and brought in materials. Seems like it's gotta be an antidote herb-collection quest."

A male adventurer was handing a cloth bag over to another receptionist. So long as he'd gathered the correct things, he was entitled to a reward.

"Please handle these." The receptionist turned around and gave the satchel to another man.

We followed that man to a different room, where he inspected the herbs. It seemed he was looking over the materials and, as I studied what he was doing, the examiner lifted his head from his work.

"Miliaaaaa, who's this guy?"

"This is Mr. Roland. It's his first day of work. Mr. Roland, this is Mr. Maurey."

"Nice to meet you," I said.

"Hmm… You have adventurer experience?" Maurey asked.

"No, I do not."

"Bold of you to work here when you haven't got any experience, don't you think? Right, Milia?"

Milia responded with a strained smile when pressed. "Ummm, I'm not too worried about that…especially when the same applies to me…"

"Better not get in the way of a former C-rank adventurer like me, rookie," Maurey cautioned.

"Uh-huh…," I answered ambiguously.

Milia, realizing I didn't really understand, quietly informed me that "a C-rank adventurer is a very capable, amazing person. Only around ten percent of all adventurers make C rank."

"I see."

So that made them slightly more competent amateur odd-job workers.

Milia brought over the slip for the antidote herb-collection quest. Difficulty for quests was ranked with letters, with S being the highest and F being the lowest.

F

Antidote Herb Collection

Collect thirty medicinal emogiso leaves that can be used to treat poisoning.

Reward: 5,000 rins

Clearly, Maurey was checking whether the herbs that had been brought in were the right plant.

"All right, that's exactly thirty of them."

He stood up and closed the cloth bag.

"Miss Milia, I think I saw some leaves in there that weren't emogiso. Is that all right?" I asked.

"Huh? I didn't see anything unusual…"

"Hey, what're you whispering about?" Annoyed, Maurey raised his voice and stared me down.

"There were leaves mixed in there that weren't the kind the quest asked for. That's all."

"What? You trying to nitpick my work?"

"No, I'm not nitpicking. It's the truth."

"You know what, I did this quest all the time when I was an adventurer. I've checked them emogiso leaves more times than I can count since I started working here, too. You better not butt in when you don't even have the experience to back it up, rookie."

Milia, who was in a fluster, cautiously whispered to me, "Mr. Roland, if you're not certain, you really shouldn't say anything…"

"Fine. Then I'll check them again," Maurey replied in a huff.

"I've seen a lot of these leaves in my day, and I've got a Plant Master qualification, too."

*The hell is that?* I thought.

As if on cue, Milia said, "A group that oversees all the Adventurers Guilds called the Adventurer Association created the Plant Master qualification for staff members."

Basically, it was a kind of certification that meant someone knew a lot about plants.

"...Hey, if you're going to apologize, now's the time to do it," Maurey chided.

"Please go ahead and check them again," I insisted.

"Tsk." Maurey clicked his tongue and emptied the bag, scattering the leaves all over the table.

"See? No matter how you look at them, they're still emogiso leaves."

"It seems you weren't looking closely at their bottom sides, then."

"...Uh."

Based on Maurey's reaction, it was obvious that he wasn't unaware of the existence of look-alike plants.

That, or...he'd known and still done it anyway.

I picked up a few of the fronds and showed the other two their undersides.

"There are some with small black spots and some without. Though they look exactly alike from the front, the ones with the spots are a weed called selily. It doesn't have antidotal properties."

"Really? That's a first for me. Ummm, so then...one, two... that's half of them! Only half of them are emogiso!"

When Milia reexamined the leaves, Maurey averted his gaze. It looked like he was in hot water.

"If you're going to brag and claim you're a professional, then I really can't applaud you for doing such a shabby job," I declared.

In my old line of work, any sort of mismanagement could prove fatal.

"Guh… Uggghhhh… But you're just a rookie!"

"And what does that have to do with anything?"

Maurey flung his arm out in an attempt to grab me. *He's getting hostile… How absurd.* Even the demon lord hadn't been able to touch a hair on my head. After I swiftly evaded, Maurey lost his balance and collapsed onto the ground.

"Um, so could you tell me—are C-rank adventurers *supposed* to be skilled?" I asked.

"Urk." Maurey, face red, stood up and left the room.

Milia let out a sigh of relief. "We were able to avoid an error because of you, Mr. Roland. I'm so impressed you knew that! That was great!"

I shook my head. "Mr. Maurey should be the one thanking me. That was close. Really close," I said.

"Oh, it was?? Was it that bad??"

"Yes, Miss Milia. To fail at your job means death."

"No it doesn't!"

"Huh?"

"Why are you acting legitimately confused about that?"

*Failures aren't fatal here…?*

Often, assassination attempts ended in failure when someone other than the target, such as an escort or guard, suspected that something was amiss. This led to a confrontation. At best, the hired killer would be murdered on the spot. At worst, they'd be captured.

First, the assassin would be tortured in the hope they'd give up the name of their employer. Regardless of the outcome, the assassin doesn't make it out of that situation in one piece. Squealing meant no one would ever trust them again. Silence meant they'd be subjected to more painful torture.

Either way, a captured assassin's career was over.

It was the same if they were spotted and fled the scene. They'd lose trust, and the target would grow far more cautious.

Nothing but drawbacks.

"Um, so what about torture…? Or poison…?" I asked.

"Why're you spouting all those disturbing words?"

Milia's eyes went wide. Evidently, nothing was going to happen to Maurey.

I'd never experienced failure. But in the event of the unthinkable, I had a poison-filled suicide capsule hidden away in my mouth. At the moment of capture, I'd kill myself.

I thought that those who considered themselves professionals would've done the same.

"I'm a bit surprised, but it seems that conventional wisdom differs by trade," I admitted.

"That's so funny. Mr. Roland, you're such an oddball." Milia giggled.

◆

Milia suddenly offered to prep a chair for my work space. Maurey, having returned, motioned with his chin. "The rookie can sit over there, can't he? You better not get in anyone's way."

It was a seat next to the window that was piled high with documents, among other things.

Earlier, Milia had told me that Maurey had been here longer than us and that we were all going to be working together from now on. As such, she'd asked that we try to get along.

"I'll help you with cleaning off the desk!"

"Milia, you don't have to do that for this guy. It's obvious the branch manager is gonna can him anyway."

If Maurey's claim was anything to go by, the branch manager seemed like a pretty ruthless boss.

"Oh, but..."

"Don't worry your pretty little head. Hey, come help me with my work, will you?"

"Ummm..."

After I nodded that it was okay, Milia gave a small bow and went to lend Maurey a hand.

"Keeping things organized... That seems nice and *normal*."

"What did you say was *normal*?"

Hearing a familiar voice, I looked down at my feet and spotted Rila.

*Where'd she come from?*

"What are you doing here?" I asked.

"What else? I'm here to mock you."

"Nice personality you've got there."

"I am the demon lord, after all." Rila slowly waved her black tail under the desk. "I cannot fathom anything stranger than a legendary assassin toiling away for a monthly salary of a mere one hundred and fifty thousand rins."

I suppose Rila just didn't know what to do with her time now that she was a cat.

As I sorted documents, Rila and I held a hushed conversation. "I'm not an assassin anymore. I'm not going to compare my previous occupation with this one."

"Oh-ho, that is a decent thing for a killing machine who sheds neither blood nor tears to say."

"Hmph. It's only natural, since I'm *normal* now."

"That conceit truly is disagreeable."

I took another look at the other staff members who were hard at work. Excluding Milia and Maurey, there were only ten people in the building. It was a pretty small guild.

Desks were grouped into fours, and each person had their own. There were three reception windows, two of which were currently busy.

Hanging on the wall was a bulletin board where quests that anyone could take were posted. I overheard some light chatter from adventurers who stood in front of it.

"Did you hear about the hero who brought down the demon lord?"

"Yeah, I heard. Looks like we won't be having any big wars for a while."

"True, but monster-slaying quests are fewer these days, too. Things might be tough for us."

"Got that right."

This town was far from the front lines and free from the ravages of war. Compared to settlements that were more likely to be raided, there wasn't much in the way of a sense of crisis around here. While I was riffling through papers, Almelia and the others from the party of heroes were probably busy with their triumph parade and celebratory party in the capital.

"Are you sure you're fine with them believing that the hero defeated me?" Rila asked.

"Yeah, I don't care about prestige or recognition. The moment I made a name for myself, I'd be a failure as an assassin."

"Hmph, I suppose that makes you top-notch, then?"

"Killing a target came as easy as breathing. It was dull, bereft of any sense of opportunity or crisis. That's all it was."

"What a waste," Rila muttered and curled up into a ball.

Right as I finished straightening up most of the things left on and around the desk, Milia took notice and said, "You're sure quick at cleaning, Mr. Roland."

"No…I'm just *normal* at it."

"Huh? Why are you grinning…? Well, never mind. It's lunch break, so let's eat together."

Maurey glanced over and stood up, then headed outside through the back exit.

"You didn't bring your own lunch, right? In that case, I'll give you half of mine. ♪" Milia offered this cheerily.

"No, I couldn't do that. I'll find something to eat outside," I replied.

*Meow, meow*, Rila agreed from under the desk. She wasn't about to risk speaking in front of other people, after all.

There was a place I frequented nearby, so I left the guild and headed over there. Along the way, however, two men and a woman—all of whom looked to be adventurers—blocked the road.

"Hey, dude, where do you think you're going?" one of them asked.

"I'm on my way out…for lunch."

"Spare us a moment, will ya?"

"We heard you're the one who scrutinized our quest. That right?"

*I see.*

These were the ones who'd brought in that emogiso. Maurey probably had some sort of connection with these people. Normally, I didn't think adventurers should've known who'd be examining the materials they brought in.

"'Cause of you, we got a quest failure."

If Maurey had some kind of deal with these three, he was probably watching from somewhere nearby… *There we go.* I spotted Maurey observing us from a spot a short ways away. Apparently, he wanted me out of the picture. If I fought back, I was sure the three adventurers would simply spread some lie about me starting the hostilities or the like.

I needed this to end peacefully.

"Who you lookin' at?" one of the adventurers prodded.

"I'm going to eat lunch, so I'd appreciate it if you could take this up with me after work," I said. "See you later," I added, trying to pass the trio by. Unfortunately, one of them grabbed me by the shoulder.

"*See you later*?! Think you're better than us, do you?"

A fist came flying toward me.

The man's wide hook had obviously seen some scuffles, but not proper battle.

He was slow.

*I need to hurry and resolve this peacefully.*

Attempting to evade his attacks would take time, and trying to counter would give the three reason to spread unsavory rumors that they'd been beaten up by a guild employee.

That being the case, the best possible thing was to make sure it was clear that I hadn't committed any violent acts. I considered allowing the punch to hit me. If I did so, though, these adventurers would likely look down on the guild staff and continue to cause trouble.

That wouldn't do.

Much like with beasts, if a person got hurt doing something, they'd develop an amount of aversion to that action.

Right as the man's fist was about to hit my cheek, I shifted slightly and took the hit on my head.

*Crunch!*

I heard a strange noise go through my skull. The bones in the attacker's hand were unexpectedly weak. Based on that sound, they'd definitely broken.

"Ah! Ah, ughhhhhh...guh..."

The adventurer held his hand and started to tear up.

Based on his reaction, the bone might've been sticking out of the back of his palm.

"Doctorrrrr!" The man ran off with tears in his eyes.

I hadn't meant to take it that far.

I suppose that was a pretty terrible thing to do to an amateur.

One of the other adventurers came at me with a mid-kick.

I didn't mind taking it, but my lunch break lasted only for so long. I needed to hurry and eat, since I wanted to go back to my *normal job*.

At the same time, I still couldn't use violence, however.

Maurey was watching.

I invoked my skill, planning to give Maurey a bout of "anemia."

In an instant, I sped forward.

Maurey was still staring intently at where I'd been standing in the street.

I stood behind him and lightly tapped his neck. He slumped on the spot.

"Huh...? Where did that guy—?"

Having noticed my disappearing right in front of his eyes, the adventurer who'd tried to kick me was glancing around.

Again, I invoked my skill. I was going to give this guy a bout of "anemia," too.

In the same way I had with Maurey, I instantly approached the man and made him faint.

It might've been going too far using my skill on amateurs, but I did it to make sure things resolved in the simplest way possible.

"Wh-what are you...?! Th-there's no way you're just a regular guild employee!" The unyielding female adventurer pointed at me.

From her perspective, I'd teleported in the blink of an eye. It was no wonder she was on her guard.

"No, I am a very *normal* new employee."

"L-liar. Some random guild staffer couldn't possibly move like tha—"

It'd mean trouble if she created a commotion in a town thorough-fare. I took the ruffled woman over to an alleyway. Unable to keep up with the pace at which I carried her, she looked around in surprise.

"Huh, where are we?"

"What just happened stays between you and me..."

I pushed her against the wall and stared intently into her eyes.

Her face flushed, but she didn't budge. Apparently, she wasn't planning on trying to escape my restraint.

"But I might let word about you slip somewhere..."

Even if she did say anything, the only thing she knew for certain was that I was powerful. I didn't want to take any chances with rumors, however.

"What do I need to do to keep you quiet?"

When I asked her that, she glanced up at me, the obvious lust in her gaze a full-blown invitation.

# ◆Maurey◆

I came to.

*Damn.* I'd only walked here to sneak a peek while that rookie Roland was getting a little roughed up.

*When did I fall asleep...?*

The three adventurers and that rookie were now gone. I could hear what sounded like somebody slapping raw hamburger patties into shape coming from a nearby alley.

"...Huh?"

When I glanced around the corner, I saw my sweet Tanya. She was half-naked, her white buttocks were out, and she was panting in short breaths like a dog.

*...HUH?! T-Tanya! A-and the rookie...! Wh-whaaat? This can't be right...?*

I meant to take him to pound town, but this wasn't what I had in mind.

I—I didn't understand what was going on. When I'd come to and looked into the alleyway, the two of them were...

*How the hell did things end up like this?!*

What the hell had happened while I was out?!

Damn it, damn it, damn it, freaking damn it...!

Tanya... I loved you just as much as Milia...!

On top of that, she was doing it with that rookie creep.

And here she never let me have a round with her...

Seemingly enraptured, Tanya said between heaving breaths, "Ohhh, mister... This might be the best I've ever had..."

I didn't want to be, but...I was turned on... What the hell...?!

I—I just couldn't take my eyes off it...

In the end, I watched until the finale... I couldn't help it.

After that, I went to the bathroom and was consequently a little late to the afternoon shift.

After my lunch break, Milia taught me the duties of the Adventurers Guild. Apparently, those without any noteworthy skills started at the reception desks. Getting a different post was possible if you received a qualification from the Adventurer Association, like that incompetent Maurey.

"So? How is he doing?" Iris, the one who'd interviewed me, came by. Her hair fluttered with her sauntering approach.

"Oh, B-Branch Manager! Th-thank you for all your hard work."

Milia bowed her head in a fluster. "Mr. Roland is quirky and says some odd things, but he's doing great! He soaks up everything like a sponge and is such a joy to teach. ♪"

"Is he? That's good, then." Iris spoke in a cool and collected manner.

Just by making an appearance, Iris had made the atmosphere of the place stiffen. I hadn't realized it because of the way our initial meeting had gone, but based on how Milia was acting, Iris really did seem like a ruthless boss.

That was curious.

She'd been reduced to trembling when I'd snatched off her underwear and then put them back on.

"Roland, I have a low tolerance for mistakes. Make sure you don't ever forget that."

"How are your delicates doing today?"

The moment I said that, Iris put her hands on her behind.

"Um! Uh… Th-they're fine! Are you t-trying to tease me…?!"

"Well, it'd be a delicate situation if you weren't wearing any at all, wouldn't it?"

"Grrr…!" Iris's face turned red again.

All around us, the other staff members were whispering to one another.

"Did the branch manager lose her cool…?"

"Who's that new guy…?"

That happened to jog my memory about something from earlier. "So according to Milia, it seems that failure doesn't result in death. Is that right, Branch Manager?"

"…Huh? Of course it doesn't."

Despite having said that she didn't tolerate mistakes, she sure seemed lenient.

"Make sure you memorize that." Iris motioned with her chin to a nearby employee manual and then left the office.

I flipped through the booklet and memorized the information written there—not as words but as images. In my previous line of work, I'd had to memorize building blueprints in mere seconds. As such, committing things to memory was pretty easy.

"I'll handle the adventurers, so for the time being, please observe how I do things." Milia huffed as though she was filled with determination and sat down. "Right now, your job is to learn, Mr. Roland."

I'd already memorized everything, though...

Then again, Milia, a more senior colleague, had given me an order, so I couldn't say no.

A man in his mid-thirties with a five-o'clock shadow sat down across from her.

Milia bowed her head.

"Welcome. Are you looking for a quest today? I see. In that case, please present your adventurer permit."

She really knew her stuff. What she was saying matched the script in the manual perfectly.

Likewise, the man handed over the necessary documentation like he'd done it a million times.

It was the first time I'd seen any such forms. *So this is an adventurer permit...*

The little card was about the size of a palm. The man's rank, name, number of accepted quests per rank, and number of successful quests per rank were listed in the upper left.

"…"

The man started blinking rapidly.

"Okay, you're a D-rank adventurer. What type of quest are you looking for today?" Milia asked.

A slight sigh escaped the man's lips, almost like he was relieved.

"…Right, a D-rank quest, please. Something I can finish before the end of the day."

"I see. Please wait one moment." Milia swiveled her chair around and searched through the shelf behind the reception desk for a quest that matched what the man was looking for. "See that, Mr. Roland? You do it like this. Find a quest suitable to the adventurer and present it to them… Right, I think this one will do just fine."

Milia pulled out a quest slip and nodded as though to affirm her decision.

Then she checked the adventurer's permit one more time.

*Something's definitely off.*

"Would you let me take a look at that?" I asked.

"Huh? You mean at the adventurer permit? Sure you can," Milia replied.

Taking a moment to scrutinize the card, I discovered a faint trace of magic on it.

"This is a fake," I declared.

"Huh? Whaaaaaat?!"

Adventurer permits were made out of a magic-repellent material so that quest achievements and ranks couldn't be faked.

At least, that's what had been written in the manual.

That's why I'd found it odd that there were traces of magic on this one.

"Traces of magic? That can't be possible... Oh. There are. They're so faint, though; I'm surprised you noticed," Milia said.

"That man was cycling between being nervous and relaxed, so I thought something must have been amiss," I explained.

"*Nervous and relaxed*, you say? Hmm."

Milia didn't appear to get it.

She glanced at the man and lowered her voice. "But why would he use a forgery? ...Does he really want to go on adventures that badly?"

He didn't look the type, but the reason was probably even simpler than that. In the manual, there'd been conditions for taking on quests. One of them was...

"Felons can't become adventurers."

Under typical circumstances, anyone who passed an exam could become an adventurer. There were some exceptions, however. The wavelengths of a person's mana were as unique as fingerprints, and they couldn't be changed.

That was why there was a mana measurement to check an applicant's wavelengths during the adventurer exam. If someone had been previously registered for a felony, regardless of whether they changed their appearance or name, the guild would find out the person was a criminal. Such a regulation was less about the Adventurers Guild and more about the clients.

"Hey, what're you gossipin' about? Hurry up and do your job!"

The man had practically shouted, earning him the attention of everyone in the room.

"Oh! Um! Th-th-th-th-this is a forgery, isn't it?! You can't use a forgery!" Milia stated rather nervously.

Judging by the man's reaction to Milia's accusation, it was hard to tell whether he was grasping at straws or had just lost it. "What're you saying?! You spout that crud, and I'll hack ya to pieces! Got that?"

"Uhhhhh... But it... Th-there are traces of magic on it, so...I thought that maybe it was a forgery..."

"You an idiot? It's natural for a permit to get a li'l roughed up and dirty!"

While that wasn't necessarily wrong, it didn't mean there'd be traces of magic on any of the cards—if they were real, of course.

"Uhhh... I suppose...that could be the case..."

As Milia floundered, Maurey spoke up from behind her. "Milia, just apologize—go on. It'll all blow over if you do."

Milia bowed her head after hearing Maurey's suggestion.

"I—I am so sorry for my rudeness..."

"You think apologizing's gonna cut it?!"

The man's hollering nearly brought Milia to tears.

As though asking what to do next, Milia looked back at Maurey. She signaled for Maurey to come over and help her out, but her senior colleague merely turned his eyes away.

"Didn't you say it would blow over...?" Milia asked.

"You just didn't apologize *the right way*, Milia. I never told you to do it like that..."

"Whaaa...?"

*I see.* If we didn't run a tight ship on our side, malcontents would have a field day with the place. Unwilling to remain a bystander, I decided to step in. "Just to be sure, sir, we will check whether your permit is genuine."

"Hmph. Fine, try it. And what'll you do if you're wrong?"

Before anyone could answer, I ignited my fingertips using magic to burn the permit I'd taken from Milia.

I saw the man grin. "No use trying that! My card's the real deal!"

A faint iridescent film enveloped the little thing. That meant I was dealing with a high-level Barrier—a type of protective magic. If the permit was made of real magic-resistant material, the man wouldn't have even been able to cast a Barrier on it. It seemed he hadn't realized that contradiction.

I decided to educate him. When I increased the power of my fire, the card was engulfed in roaring flames.

"Ahhhhhh! That thing cost me a hundred fifty thousand! Oh."

"The sale of adventurer permits is strictly forbidden. Peddled or traded permits are invalid. Naturally, magically ignitable forgeries are no good, either."

"I had 'em cast some high-level defense magic on that thing! It shouldn't have gone up from some little finger fireworks show!" the man shouted, incredulous.

Just because I was an assassin, that didn't mean magic was beyond my capabilities. Depending on the situation, it'd make for an ideal *termination*. If I could stab someone to death with a dagger, I could plow them through with magic. Admittedly, I didn't have much experience with the latter method, but I was skilled enough to at least try it.

...Regardless, this guy was soft.

Evidently, an adventurer (or someone claiming to be one) could manage only a pretty obvious forgery...

Failure as an assassin meant death. If it were me, I wouldn't have used an imitation. I would've stealthily snuffed someone and used *their* card. Adventurer permits didn't detail the holder's appearance. As long as no one in the guild recognized the person, they wouldn't be exposed.

Work was in the details.

It was the man's own fault for doing a half-baked job. Just by killing a single adventurer, he would've been able to obtain a genuine permit that he'd never have gotten his hands on otherwise. It seemed a cheap price to pay, but perhaps he just didn't have the stomach for it? I didn't know what crime he'd been convicted of, but he was no professional. That much was certain.

"You're lucky you're an adventurer. Had you been an assassin, you would have been dead by now," I said casually.

"Huh?"

"W-we have to tell the Order of Chivalry—"

When Milia said that, the man turned around and scrambled toward the exit.

We were likely going to have to question him about where he had acquired the forged papers. I leaped over the counter, caught the man, and pinned him to the floor.

"G-guuuuuuuuuh..."

*Clap, clap.* Applause broke out in the guild.

*Hmm? Is that for me?*

I tied up the man with a rope and handed him off to the Order of Chivalry knights who came by. After explaining the situation to them, we left it in their hands.

"Mr. Roland, that was amazing. You caught him lickety-split.

Also, you really helped me out there. Thank you so much. I was so frightened…"

"Not at all. I'm glad nothing further happened."

"It's only your first day…yet you're so laid-back and reliable… What a curious person."

Milia nodded a few times and gazed at me, enraptured.

# 5

# I Want to Live in a Normal House

Tomorrow was a holiday.

Milia and Maurey were discussing it in the office.

"Miliaaa, isn't it a day off tomorrow? Let's eat out together. It's been such a long time since we've had a break, right? I know this great place…"

Milia smiled awkwardly at the invitation.

"Uhhh, well… I have plans, so…I'm sorry."

I busied myself filing documents as I considered what to do with the day off myself.

"Mr. Roland, where do you live? Are you on the eastern side?" Milia asked, making her way over to my desk.

The east side of the town was mostly residential and relatively quiet.

"Where do I live…? I stay at an inn every night."

"Whaaat?! Y-you must be rich…"

"You think so?"

"Yes, I mean, normally, people live in houses that are within commuting distance of their workplace."

When she hit me with that bombshell, I automatically parroted back, "People *normally* live in houses that are within commuting distance of their workplace?!"

I had a house in the mountains, but I usually went there only once every couple of months. Perhaps it was more appropriate to call it a rest stop than a house. After mulling it over for a moment, I came to the realization that I'd never had a fixed workplace before.

I'd had targets instead of an office.

Usually, I took up residence wherever the target was. From a place in their neighborhood, I could conduct a detailed investigation—what time they woke up in the morning, what they ate for breakfast, what they did for work, when they went home, whether they took detours, how many times they went to the bathroom, how many women they slept with, what quirks they had, their family, their friends, their lovers...

Once I'd researched every aspect of the target, I would rule out any options beyond my capability. Overestimating my abilities and failing as a result was less than ideal, after all. The same went for the battlefield. The cowardly lived longer than the gallant.

The option to live near my workplace had never even crossed my mind.

"I suppose it makes sense to live close by if you have one fixed workplace..."

"Mr. Roland, if you keep spending your nights at an inn, you'll end up losing most of your salary to lodging fees. Oh, or are you skimping on your meals? That's no good. You need to make sure you eat up. Otherwise you won't have any energy."

"Somewhat of an opinionated damsel, isn't she?" came a new voice.

"Huh? Did you hear a woman's voice just now?" Milia asked.

"I didn't hear anything," I insisted.

As usual, Rila was curled up under the desk at my feet.

"I suppose…a house would seem more *normal*."

"It wouldn't *seem* normal; it *is* normal."

That settled it. Searching for one was my next goal.

"Oh, if you'd like, I can show you around the town and give you a tour of some vacant places. ♪ This is my hometown, so I know it like the back of my hand."

"So it is. In that case, please do show me around."

"I hope it is an abode befitting my presence," Rila commented, letting another mutter slip.

As I spied Maurey looking peeved from the corner of my eye, Milia and I made plans on where and when we would meet tomorrow. I wondered what had happened to her other plans. When Rila and I got home, I voiced my confusion on the matter.

"You should have been able to ascertain what it meant based on the flow of the conversation," Rila explained. "Her so-called plans were a roundabout means of turning that other man down."

"I see. By doing that, she can refuse him without aggravating the situation."

"There you have it," Rila said.

Apparently, claiming to have plans was a regular practice among women. Ladies sure had it tough.

When Rila and I went to meet Milia out in front of the Adventurers Guild the next day, I was surprised to find she was already there.

"Sorry for being late."

"Not at all—I was just early. You're right on time. Oh, a kitty! Is she yours?"

"Yes. I'd like to show her our new home as well."

"That's an excellent idea."

When Milia tried petting her, Rila turned her face away and hid behind me. Milia's action was harmless, but Rila had no intention of humoring the girl.

Following after Milia, we began the house-hunting journey.

"My family has lived in this town forever, so I pretty much know all the vacant houses and who owned them. What kind of place are you looking for?"

"That's obvious. A *normal* house," I replied.

"…Um… I'm not planning to show you mansions or anything, rest assured."

"A quiet place would be most appreciated."

"All right! …Wait? Was that your voice just now…Mr. Roland?"

"Yes, it was."

It had actually been Rila, but I wasn't about to offer up that information.

"Uhhhh?" Milia cocked her head to the side. "Well, okay."

The first place she showed us was a single-building house in a residential district on the eastern side.

"My place is pretty close, barely even a ten-minute walk away! This house hasn't been empty for very long, so it's in good shape. Also, w-we could walk to work together…hee-hee."

The building was surrounded by other residences. While it had no yard, it was a tidy enough spot. After taking it in, Rila shook her head. It seemed this house did not please the great and powerful demon lord.

"Please show me the next one," I said.

"Uhhh…sure…"

Milia then began whispering some complaints to herself—"I thought that was a pretty nice house... It seemed like a good place..."—as she continued on to the next available home.

The second house seemed to be on the outskirts of town.

Even from afar, it was easy to pick out because there was so little else around. The yard was so overgrown with weeds that I couldn't even see the ground.

"The owner apparently used to be an adventurer, but it seems to have been unoccupied for a loooong time. It's not unusual for adventurers to go missing, so most likely..."

If the person had been missing for years, it was easy to imagine the end of Milia's sentence, even if I hadn't been working at a guild.

This building was a little larger than the place we'd seen in the residential district. The only thing nearby was a small stream. It was quiet, and the passing breeze was pleasant. Occasionally, I could hear the running water of the creek. The only real drawbacks were that the house was rather old, and it was situated far from most things in town.

Rila's tail was waving back and forth. I'd noticed it only recently, but that seemed to indicate she was in a good mood.

"Let's take a quick peek inside."

The moment that Milia touched the door, I felt a restless presence. Rila's ears likewise stood at attention.

It was the presence of an undead-type monster.

"Please wait here, Miss Milia."

"Huh? I suppose I can..."

Though many of the guild staff were former adventurers, such wasn't true for all of them. Milia was obviously just a regular civilian.

The unlocked door creaked open at my tugging on the handle. Thieves could've been using this place as their hideout.

It was a lot more spacious than it appeared from the outside. Sunlight streamed in from the windows, making the place relatively bright. This only made it harder to see in the dark corners, however.

"Knave, it is this room," Rila said.

"Right."

Something like smoke was gushing from a door in the back.

"An ordinary human would hardly be able to stay in their right mind... Obviously, you're an exceptional case, though."

"You mean *normal*, don't you?"

"What is normal about you?"

Entering the room where the vapor was coming from, I was immediately greeted by something that looked like the floating top half of a human. Its body was partially transparent. The creature's nearly human face was home to a single, dark-yellow-colored eye. This monster was known as a dark plasma.

"MrrrrrrGHHHH!"

Dark plasmas were troublesome opponents that consumed vitality.

I'd fought such things several times before; it was fastest to defeat one using magic... This was supposed to be my new home, though. I didn't like the idea of risking collateral damage from a stray shot.

"So what shall you do?" Rila inquired.

"Just watch."

I gathered mana into my left arm, wreathing my forearm in magic.

"Oh, I had no idea you could be so skillful…"

"MrrAAAAAAGH!"

With no small amount of agility, the dark plasma came flying at me.

"Hmph!"

*BWOOSH!*

My left arm bored a clean hole right through the dark plasma's chest.

"Aaaaaahhh…"

Wailing its last, agonizing breath, my opponent dropped the mana stone it had used as a catalyst. The dark plasma's form dimmed until it had completely disappeared. Excess mana seemed to stream from my arm. That quickly came to a halt after I stopped routing mana through my arm, however.

"Among demonkind, cladding a part of your body with mana is a trick we refer to as Magi Raegas."

"That's a pretty over-the-top name for just wearing mana."

"It is because few grasp it. It is only natural for it to have an aggrandized name."

"Seems a lot more demonkind are unadept than I'd assumed."

"What do you mean? It is you who are the aberration."

I really did feel more at home in battle than working as a guild employee. Maybe it was just because I'd gotten so used to it.

After I defeated the dark plasma and took a look around the house, I returned to Milia.

"How was it?" she asked.

"I'll take it. It's quiet and just right for me," I answered.

"I'm glad. Well then, how about we go back to town? I'll help you move."

"I don't have any belongings. It's fine."

"Huh?"

"I'm going to clean the house and tend the yard, so that's it for today."

"Huh? A-already? I was hoping we could at least have lunch together...," Milia mumbled. Then, as though something had suddenly come to her mind, she clapped her hands together. "I-in that case, I'll make lunch and bring it over! While I'm doing that, you can clean, Mr. Roland."

She dashed off without even waiting for my reply.

"Seems she has taken a liking to you," Rila observed.

"You think so? I hadn't even thought of lunch, so it honestly is a help."

I looked around inside the house again. Excluding the living room and kitchen, there were four rooms. There was no end to the dust, but it seemed like it'd be a usable enough place after a good cleaning.

I touched Rila's collar. Her body glowed, and she reverted to her original form. We'd been close to each other at the moment of transformation, and it'd forced Rila's back against a wall. Our faces were almost touching.

"Rila...let's do it."

After blinking several times, Rila blushed and turned away.

"W-we cannot... Though...it is a new home...and we are alone... W-we have no idea when the damsel might come back..."

"We'll finish before she returns."

Rila turned her face toward me.

"…Nn."

She squeezed her eyes shut and puckered her lips.

"Hmm? You'll be in charge of the wet rooms—I'm leaving the kitchen, bath, and toilet to you. I'll clean the rest."

"…"

"Open your eyes. Get going. Time is of the essence."

Rila trembled for a moment and then hit me square in the chest.

"Screw you!" Rila stomped loudly down the hall. "*Ngaaaah?! Th-the floor has caved in! Hurry and get over here, knave! I—I cannot move…*"

"You're such a handful."

Rila's head was the only thing above the broken floorboards when I came to pull her out. With parts of the house in such bad shape, it was all I could do to repair them as they demanded.

After the two of us went about our cleaning for a bit, Milia returned holding a basket in both her hands.

"Whoa…! Mr. Roland, it looks so much cleaner."

"Well, I didn't do it alone. Let me introduce you. This is Rila, the demon who assisted me."

"Hmph." Rila arrogantly puffed up her chest. "My name is Rileyla. However, I shall *allow* you to call me Rila. It appears you're the one looking after Roland during his work hours. Is that correct?"

"Hello…my name is Milia McGuffin. I'm Mr. Roland's colleague."

Most demons were affiliated with the demon lord army and rightfully feared by humans. It would've been completely understandable if Milia had been scared, too.

"Miss Milia, it's all right. Despite being a demon, she can't use magic."

"Oh, she can't? That's a relief."

The largest differences between demons and humans were the discrepancies in magical abilities and magical skills. Demons were superior in both.

Rila dug right into the lunch that Milia had set on the table.

"Hmph. Acceptable."

"H-hey! But I only made enough for Mr. Roland and me!"

"Grrr," Milia whispered into my ear as she pouted. "What is with this pompous woman?"

"I met her while I was traveling, and we ended up getting close…"

That much wasn't a lie. I could've told Milia that Rila was the demon lord, but it seemed unlikely that she'd believe such a story.

"I am not especially partial to this; however…it's not terrible. You may bring more again."

"She's totally mocking me!"

The three of us enjoyed the meal while Milia fumed over Rila's teasing. It seemed Milia had made everything herself. Even someone like me, who couldn't tell the difference between good and bad, could easily recognize that it was fine home cooking.

"Once we finish, I can help you clean the place up," Milia offered.

"We have sufficient hands here. You may skip along home," Rila stated.

"Not! A! Chance!"

As someone who knew Rila's true identity, it was a little funny to watch the demon lord and a small-town girl like Milia stare each other down.

"The more people, the better. Please help us, Miss Milia."

"Gladly!"

Apparently, Milia was quite good at cleaning.

"Hey, Miss Prima Donna, looks like things aren't going smoothly for you. You're not inept at cleaning, by any chance, are you? Pfft!"

"I hail from nobility. I could clean a house in mere moments if I summoned some beasts to do it for me. Just watch—'*From the shadows, come, my companions. By this principle, manifest yourself upon this contract*'!"

"…Ha-ha. Nothing happened. What was that just now? Were you trying to imitate someone or what? Oh my, that's odd. I didn't even feel the *m* in magic from that. Pfft!"

"Why, you little! You dare make a mockery of me…? I will not forgive this, damsel…!"

The two women seemed to be having fun.

Surprisingly, Rila put some effort into cleaning, likely because Milia had riled her up.


Thanks to everyone's efforts, the place looked noticeably better by nightfall.

"Oh, would you like to have dinner at my house?" Milia asked.

I was thinking of just going to a restaurant, but there weren't any near my new house.

"I will be abstaining from this invitation," Rila declared.

"I see," said Milia. "Then let's be on our way, Mr. Roland."

"In that case, I will take you up on your offer," I replied.

"Okay. ♪"

Rila growled and started to rock the chair she was sitting in until it clattered. In contrast, Milia waved her hand at Rila with a cheerful smile as she and I made our departure.

"I forbid you from staying out too late."

I hesitated over whether to turn Rila into a cat, but I decided she was fine as she was. It wasn't as though anyone was going to pay the house a visit.

"All right," was the last thing I said as I left my new home behind.

"When I went back to my place to make lunch, I told my dad about your house... There's apparently a rumor about a strange monster haunting that building... You haven't had any trouble, have you? I know it's a bit late to be bringing that up, but I was so worried..."

"Ah, that. I already cleaned it up."

"Y-you cleaned it up...?"

"It was a dark plasma. It seems it used this as a catalyst and had taken up residence in that house."

I handed over the mana stone to Milia.

"A-a dark plasma...?! That kind of monster would warrant a B-rank solo quest!"

"It would?"

I really didn't know the criteria for what made a monster weak or strong, it seemed. When it came to opponents I'd defeated in war, I'd memorized their weaknesses, so I had no issues dealing with them.

"When you say you *cleaned it up*, you don't mean that you defeated it...? Ahhh..." Milia's jaw dropped, and she blinked a few times in rapid succession. "But I was sure I'd heard they were resistant to physical attacks."

"I stuck my arm right through its chest."

"What is going on…? But they're mostly intangible… Mr. Roland, you're not actually really talented or something, are you??"

"No, I'm just *normal.*"

"It sure doesn't seem that way…"

Amid our chatter, we soon arrived at Milia's house. Her mother, a kind-looking woman, had just finished making dinner inside.

"Mom, this is Mr. Roland. We work together."

"Oh my, hello. Thank you for helping out my daughter."

"Not at all. Milia's the one helping me out."

As I waited in the seat that was offered to me, Milia's father came by and gave me a simple greeting. We talked about the guild, the adventurers, and my life before starting work at the Adventurers Guild. Conversation during the meal was quite varied. Milia and her parents had never lived outside the town before, so they were taken in by my stories.

"We live ordinary lives in a normal town, so I'm sure we must seem boring in your eyes, Roland."

"Not at all."

The atmosphere was warm, almost bashfully so.

"I think it's quite wonderful that you live this way."

The parents exchanged a look and smiled awkwardly at my honest remark.

"We're just a normal household—nothing special," the mother said.

*I see…so this is the fabled* normal household…

"We come home after working at the kind of jobs you could find anywhere. Then we eat, sleep, and go back to work… Our days are exceedingly mundane like that, Roland."

They might've thought it boring, but depending on the location, I'd say it was a rare way of living. With the war over, there were likely to be more and more people living this way, though.

While I was lost in thought, the dad continued. "Eventually, you find someone you get close to and marry them. Then make a house and raise the kids you have... That's how an ordinary man's normal life goes."

"*An ordinary man's normal life...?!*"

I engraved that into my memory.

*So this is the life of a* normal man...

...What profound words Milia's father had spoken to me.

I felt odd.

It was the first time I'd ever realized that such a warm place and such kind people could truly exist.

This was the *normal* I sought.

As Milia and her mother stood from their seats in order to clean up, I turned to Milia's father. "You seem quite close with your wife."

"Well...she was terrifying when I was unfaithful..." The man's eyes looked distant. "When there's an opportunity, it's in a man's nature to take it, you know?"

"So seizing upon opportunity is *normal*...?"

"Yes. I'm sure a young man like you gets many offers."

"You think so?"

This was a conversation between two men. Back on the battlefield, I'd overheard soldiers and officers saying similar sorts of things. "*I'd like to do* it *if I had the opportunity.*"

I'd thought that carnal appetite had been beget through the

unique circumstances of war, but according to Milia's father, that seemed to not be the case. That meant it was *normal* for a man...

With the night wearing on, I excused myself from Milia's home.

"I have never been made to wait so long, knave! What a favorable position you are in to deign to delay the demon lord so! I even cautioned you so strongly not to— Are you listening?!"

Rila was fuming.

She'd started telling me off the second I got home. I merely silenced her with my lips. When I asked her if she was satisfied after I did that, Rila bashfully nodded several times.

Evidently, that had put her into such a good mood that the mighty demon lord standing in my entryway looked positively thrilled.

# 6

# A Man Sees Something Through

Careful not to wake Rila as she slept next to me, I slipped out of bed. After arriving at the Adventurers Guild, I prepped for work. Truthfully, all my work amounted to was filing documents, though... Regardless, I dutifully fulfilled the obligations of my position.

"Good morning, Mr. Roland. Would you like to work the window today?" Milia offered.

"Sure. I'll take reception."

"Okay! If there's anything you're not sure about, I'll be at my desk, so just come by and ask."

"Understood."

Once the office opened, an adventurer immediately took a seat in front of me.

"I'm here for a quest today."

"Very well."

I accepted his adventurer permit and looked it over.

His name was Neal. Thirty-three years old. Rank D. He'd done quite a number of quests—mostly E- and F-rank ones. His weapon specialization was with a bow.

"What do you think of this E-rank quest?" Just as Milia had instructed, I presented Neal with a quest slip and explained the job to him.

The adventurer shook his head. "I'd like a D-rank slaying quest."

In my eyes, there wasn't much difference between E- and D-rank quests. Both were low-level. Despite not knowing much about the differences between the two ranks, D rank wasn't beyond Neal's capabilities. I searched for a new job that fit his desire.

*For an archer like this adventurer Neal, I suppose this will do.*

"A quest to 'drive back the foul killer falcon'...how does this sound?"

"Yes, I'll take that, please."

I asked the man to wait before going through formalities and heading to Milia's desk.

"What's the matter?" she asked.

"Do you think...this might be difficult for a D-rank quest?"

Adventurers could naturally take on quests of the same rank as themselves. Killer falcons differed greatly from one to the next, however. One could be a formidable opponent.

"I don't. Do you think it is...? We had another killer-falcon-slaying quest recently that was classified as a D rank."

"If the adventurer thinks he can handle it, then what's the big deal? Let 'im. Not like it goes against the rules or anything," Maurey interjected from his place sitting across from Milia.

"If you're worried, Mr. Roland, you could call it off?"

"The killer falcon could just as easily be too weak as it could be too strong. You could even say that they are the best type of monster to help build one's confidence—"

"Hey! Are you guys ignoring me?!" Maurey snapped.

I did another search through our files, but this was the only

D-rank slaying quest we had. Returning to Neal, I processed his request, and he departed the guild.

I was a bit concerned. This was the first quest and adventurer I had handled. Leaving the reception window to Milia, I stood from my seat.

As I left through the back exit, the branch manager Iris called out to me. "Where do you think you're going?"

"I plan on observing the outcome of a quest I'm responsible for. I'll be back in a bit," I replied.

"I happened to hear a little about you from the guild master… You hadn't changed your name, so it was obvious right away… You're much nicer than you've been made out to be."

"I'm just a normal guild employee now."

"…Hmm. Well, I guess I'll just happen to overlook this. Good luck."

I bobbed my head at Iris as she turned her back to me; then I left the guild behind.

I took off my glasses and put them in my pocket. According to Rila, donning or removing glasses could really change how you appeared to other people.

Heading to the area the quest slip had described, I found Neal nocking his bow on a cliff top.

"ScreeeeEEE!" A killer falcon let out a piercing cry as it circled in the air.

Recently, it had been wreaking havoc by attacking the merchants who traveled the nearby roads. That's why the slaying quest had come in. At a glance, the falcon looked pretty big. Its speed and beak strength were probably higher than average.

The arrow that Neal the adventurer let loose curved off the mark. The creature glided toward him at once upon noticing the failed attack.

"Uh, ahhhhhhhHHH?!"

Neal the adventurer threw down his weapon and wrapped his arms over his head.

The killer falcon nearly grazed him as it sped over.

*This looks precarious…*

Neal's opponent was a large killer falcon. He should have known that taking on such a foe wasn't going to be easy.

As Neal the adventurer cautiously lifted his head, he readied his bow again, aimed, gave up, aimed, gave up, and continued that pattern.

"It's difficult to tell from afar, but the killer falcon is fast enough in the air to be among the top-ten speediest monsters. It's unlikely you'd be able to hit one from the ground," I said.

"Who're you?"

"I'm a passing…adventurer."

I had come here straight after leaving the window duties to Milia. The plan was to depart right after I'd given my advice.

"While the killer falcon is a master of the skies, there *is* a moment when it's defenseless."

"There is?! When?"

"When it's hunting for its prey."

This didn't just apply to the killer falcon. Hunters were always the pursuers. It was beyond them to assume that they were the ones being hunted.

"Then I've just got to set out some bait so that when it comes to eat—"

"This creature reacts to moving things. If it hasn't been domesticated, it likely wouldn't even look at a piece of meat even if you left some out for it."

"So I need to catch a rabbit or something…but there aren't many small animals around these parts…"

"By the way, they sometimes eat humans."

"Blech!"

"You have firsthand experience with that already, though."

"What do you mean? When it dodged my arrow?"

"No, after that. It swooped down at you, didn't it?"

"Well… Huh? You don't mean—"

"That's right. It's the quickest way."

"I—I couldn't possibly! That thing was ridiculously huge and scary when it was coming at me!"

"Don't knock it until you've tried it."

"Tch…"

From many available options, Neal had chosen a bow and was currently at rank D. That meant he was most confident in battle when he was using the ranged weapon.

"This will put your archery—and your courage—to the test. If you're opposed to the idea, then go catch some wild game and bring it back here. Truthfully, though… If you don't even have enough confidence to shoot something like this down, then you might as well quit being an archer."

"All right! I'll do it! I clawed my way this far up the ranks using only my bow. I owe it to myself to try!"

It seemed he was ready.

After taking several deep breaths, Neal nocked an arrow.

While it would've been great if this shot struck the bird, it failed to find purchase. The killer falcon easily evaded it, then dived toward Neal again.

"ScreeeeEE!"

"…Ugh."

Despite being obviously flustered, Neal didn't fumble as he once again readied his bow. The look in his eyes was entirely different than it had been a moment ago. After waiting for the falcon to get close enough that he knew he wouldn't miss, Neal let his arrow fly.

The confrontation was over in an instant.

While Neal still had to overcome his fear of being charged at, his eyes seemed plenty keen.

I headed back to work without bothering to see what befell him after that first hit.


By the time I returned to the Adventurers Guild, only around an hour had passed.

I put my glasses back on and adopted a meek expression.

"Mr. Roland, are you all right?" Milia asked when she saw me. She looked almost ready to cry.

"All right…? What do you mean?"

"B-because the branch manager was just saying that you wouldn't come out of the bathroom!"

I decided to go with it.

"Yes, I'm fine. I'm feeling much better thanks to you."

"What a relief!"

Maurey interjected from the side again. "Hey, rookie, you

better not make Milia worry. Taking care of your own health's a part of your job. Right, Milia?"

"Miss Prima Donna probably forced you to eat something bizarre, right?" Milia asked.

"No, she isn't the type to do anything as laudable as cook a meal," I replied.

"…Hey, why do you two always ignore me? I'm supposed to be your senior, you know? C'mon—what's up with this??" Maurey whined.

I took back my receptionist-window duties from Milia. Later in the day, after I'd helped a few more adventurers, Neal finally made his return.

"Here is my proof of completion…a killer falcon's feather!"

I handed off the feather to the inspector for examination. It didn't take long to affirm that it had indeed come from a real killer falcon.

"Congratulations. Here is your quest reward," I said.

After conducting the proper procedures described in the manual, I handed Neal his recompense.

"I feel like I can do a lot more after this quest."

"That's good to hear. We look forward to working with you again."

When I lightly bowed my head, Neal stealthily whispered, "Thank you very much."

"What do you mean?" I asked.

"Oh, nothing."

A faint smile on his face, Neal made his exit.

I decided that next time I took off my glasses, I'd also try changing my hairstyle, too.

# 7

# The Missing Adventurer

I pressed on, moving deeper into the forest, just as the quest slip I'd memorized had indicated.

An adventurer had gone out on an E-rank quest but was taking far too long.

*"Roland, I want you to go and search for that adventurer and retrieve his permit."*

Iris had sent me out as soon as I'd come into the office that day. My job this time was to search for the missing person and bring him back, if possible. Barring that, the goal was to return with his adventurer permit.

"Mr. Roland, I baked some cookies for today. Would you care to take a break somewhere?"

Milia lightly patted her bag. She'd tagged along for my excursion.

"We haven't even been in the woods for a whole thirty minutes yet. We'll take a break later."

"Hmph, I see your head's just as full of flowers as it usually is."

Bored, Rila had also come with us today. Naturally, she was in her black-cat form.

"Mr. Roland, your kitty is sooo cute. Are you wowwied about your owner?"

*Mrowl!* Rila swung her claws at Milia and scampered away.

"Oh…she hates me…"

Rila trotted up next to my feet. In a whisper, I asked, "Are you worried about me?"

"Hmph. It would be a waste to worry about someone stronger than I am."

That much was certainly true. As for Milia, she'd come along because she'd been the one to assign the missing adventurer this quest.

"Usually, I'd leave this sort of thing to staffers who have adventurer experience, but it makes me feel like I'm not taking responsibility for things. That's why I wanted to come with you this time."

"Be that as it may, the 'picking mandarins from the citron flower' quest is only an E rank. I don't think you need to be so dutiful about this…"

Maybe Milia was getting herself worked up so she wouldn't feel too worried over the disappearance.

A week had passed since the quest report time limit. The adventurer had either encountered an unforeseen accident or chosen to go AWOL.

Abandoning a quest without permission was called going AWOL—absent without leave. Someone who abandoned a quest was never allowed to work as an adventurer again.

The mandarin of the citron flower was an ingredient required for making healing medicine. The quest slip had cited a gathering spot in the woods. Picking the fruits in some other place wasn't really an issue, but the forest was fairly close to town.

"The missing person is a boy who'd just become an E-rank adventurer recently. I wonder where he went off to… If we can't find him after searching today and tomorrow, he'll end up kicked out of the guild… And we haven't had any reports from the Adventurers Guilds in other towns, either…"

"Obviously, he is dead. Searching for a corpse is a very principled job."

"How could you say something like that?! Wait, wasn't that Miss Prima Donna's voice just now…?"

"No, that was me," I said. "It was an impersonation. Pretty good, right?"

"That's amazing! You're so talented!"

Rila snickered from her place at my feet.

"There shouldn't be anything unusual about this forest. If he got lost, we might find him resting somewhere," I continued.

"Um, uh, I'm sure there was a cave nearby—"

When Milia attempted to pull out a map, I spoke up. "I know the one you're talking about; it's this way."

"You've memorized the map?"

"Yes. I can memorize most things more or less at a glance."

"Th-that really is amazing…"

"But I also forget everything the next morning."

It was a result of my training. Retaining certain information could be dangerous.

There was a distinct restlessness in the air when we arrived at the cave. A monster or some such thing might have made a nest out of it.

"Hmm. I sense the presence of a beast-type monster. The lad may have entered without realizing it was a nest," Rila said.

"Yes, that seems plausible," I replied.

"Are you doing two roles at once…?"

"Please wait here, Miss Milia. There's likely to be a monster in there."

"Will you be all right, Mr. Roland? Isn't it dangerous?"

"That's no issue. If I don't return by the time the sun begins to set, please go back to the guild without me."

"I—I understand… H-here. Why don't you take my cookies?"

"Thank you very much."

Milia thrust the sweets toward me, and I received them gladly. As Rila and I entered the cave, I let her taste one of the confections.

"Hmm, palatable."

Ever haughty, that one.

Rila asked for a second and then a third. It seemed she had taken a liking to them. I ate one as well. It had a nice texture and wasn't too sweet—a delicious cookie.

If the information from the guild was to be believed, the forest cave wasn't supposed to be very deep.

"Ah, I smell a beast. In this season, it may be one of those…"

The overpowering and acrid smell of a wild animal buffeted my nostrils. The farther we progressed, the stronger it became.

"Grrrrrrrrrrowl…!"

*Thump, thump.* A bearlike monster barreled out from the back of the cave. Its eyes were bloodshot, and it breathed in great huffs.

"A gray bear, is it? The thing appears quite agitated."

"Rila, you look for the missing adventurer."

"If I must."

Gracefully, Rila passed right by the gray bear.

With no one else around, I faced the animal one-on-one.

"GROOOOooooooRWLLL!"

With a roar, the gray bear stood up. It rose to around six and a half feet tall.

As it swung with an arm, the biting smell of blood passed by my nose.

*FWSHT!* The beast's claws raked into the ground.

I had to admit, the attack had been fairly quick. The bear seemed more than ready to fight to the death. Had I not known much about battle, I doubt I would've made it out of the cave alive. Leaving the bear wasn't an option—it was likely to kill someone if left to its own devices.

"Hmph."

I used a karate chop to break off one of its claws.

*"Graaah?!"* The gray bear looked startled, unable to comprehend what'd just happened.

"Hmph."

This time, I sent my fist flying, aiming for its mouth.

*CRRRSH!* Several of its fangs broke.

"GRAaaah?!"

"One more."

I snapped another one of the bear's teeth, and the beast let out a thunderous howl.

"GrroooOOOOOOOOWWW!"

I'd thought my display of strength enough for the gray bear to understand that I was stronger, but it insisted on continuing to fight.

*Oh well.*

I slipped behind it and simultaneously jumped into the air. Before the bear even had the time to turn around, I delivered a blow to its neck.

"Urk..."

*THUUUD.* The gray bear collapsed on the spot.

From the shadows, a gray bear cub appeared. It seemed I had just defeated the mother.

"Cwoo..."

The cub nudged its mother with its nose. She'd been protecting her child. That explained why she had been so violent.

"Cwoo, cwoo."

"Don't worry. She's just asleep."

It was the truth. I'd been the one who'd intruded on their home, after all. I'd simply wanted to check whether the adventurer was deeper in the cave. I hadn't come here to slay anything.

I did, however, collect a severed claw and fang to prove I'd actually encountered the bear.

Hopefully, after being subjected to that much pain, the beast would remember to fear human opponents. With luck, it wouldn't try attacking any passersby from now on.

No sooner had I finished collecting what I needed than Rila came running back.

"Knave! I have found him! He is yet breathing—"

"All right, lead me to him."

"Over here," Rila said, and I ran after her. We found a boy sitting up against the back wall of the deepest chamber in the cave.

After we gave him some water, he finally opened his eyes.

"Are you guild staff...?"

Checking his adventurer permit, I confirmed that this was indeed the missing person. I had him cling to my back and exited the cave. The boy didn't seem to be sporting any particularly grievous injuries. Perhaps he'd entered without realizing it was the gray bear's lair and then had been unable to escape. Such a beast would've been too much for an E-rank adventurer to take on.

"This is the kid, right, Miss Milia? He seems a bit weak, but he should be all right."

"What a relief…" Milia let out a huge sigh.

After checking on the boy, who had fallen asleep at some point, tears formed at the corners of Milia's eyes.

"I'm so happy we've found him…I really am. Mr. Roland, thank you so much. Truly."

"You don't have to thank me. I just wondered if he might be in the cave."

"No, no. Normally, we would've called for backup and asked other adventurers to help, but you went in without paying any mind to the dangers—"

"What…?! People *normally* don't stroll into things like this…?!"

"Huh? What? I-it's all right. Everything worked out. That just means you're brave and uncompromising."

…If that was the case, then I suppose there was no harm.

"Oh, here. It's a gray bear claw and fang. It attacked me in the cave, but I taught it a swift lesson. I don't think it'll be bothering people for a while."

"A gray… What? Um, did you say a *gray bear*?!"

"Yes. That's what it was."

"Those are very savage and formidable enemies! Fighting one

is usually an A-rank slaying quest. They're known for becoming violent this time of year..."

*I see. So that's how it is.*

"It should be fine. The bear was only lashing out because it had a cub. So long as we don't intrude on its territory, it shouldn't pose any problems."

"Hwah...? Really? You sure are knowledgeable for someone who isn't an adventurer, Mr. Roland!"

"W-well...I am well traveled."

It wasn't a lie—truly, it wasn't.

When we got back to the Adventurers Guild, we first had a doctor examine the boy. Nothing seemed to be wrong with him, so we thought it was likely he'd perk up after we let him rest for a while.

"Mr. Roland rescued that boy from a cave!"

A buzz arose from the entire guild before they broke into loud applause.

"You mean that cave in the woods? You've seriously got some guts, newbie!"

"Did you really fight off a gray bear, too? Are you sure you're not an adventurer?"

Excluding Maurey, my senior colleagues gave a rough, but no less welcoming, reception.

A few days later, the boy had recovered and came by to offer his gratitude.

"I owe you my life. Thank you so much!"

"Make sure you're careful from now on."

"Yes, sir!"

I was being appreciated without having to kill anyone. Maybe this *normal* work wasn't too bad.

# 8
# We Need One More!

Most of the time, I was given filing work at the guild. Occasionally, I'd take the reception window when someone had their hands full or I'd help out with appraisal and inspection. I also would search for adventurers under Iris's instructions. Admittedly, it wasn't so much a search as it was just retrieving someone's papers.

"Hmm… This is troubling…" Milia groaned from her spot dealing with inquiries at the reception window.

She was tending to a group of three adventurers. There was a short-haired man holding a spear, another who wore robes and looked to be a cleric, and Neal, the one I'd been charged with a few days ago.

Our eyes met, and Neal slightly bowed his head in my direction.

"One more…," Milia muttered as she left her seat and came to the shelf next to my desk. She picked up the adventurer register.

"What's the matter?"

"Oh, Mr. Roland. There's a C-rank party quest, but…I haven't been able to find the number of adventurers needed."

I had her show me the quest slip. The job was driving away the monsters that had attacked a nearby village. Party quests were often larger-scale tasks that couldn't be accomplished alone. They also gave out proportionally larger rewards.

"We need one more, but today is the recruiting deadline... All of them are really fired up to take on the quest. I was the one who made them go through the hassle of grouping up. I feel bad..."

Apparently, Milia had asked all the able adventurers who'd come by today to join, but each of them had turned her down.

"Once the deadline passes, another branch takes over the recruitment—is that correct?"

"Yes, that's exactly it! I'm so impressed you've memorized all those details." Milia broke into a grin as she praised me.

"M-Mr. Roland...I mean, boss! W-would you be kind enough to join us?!" Neal the adventurer bowed his head.

"Uh, you mean me...?"

*What's this* boss *business all about? I'm pretty sure he's older than I am.*

"I'm sure Mr. Roland could...but I've never heard of a staff member helping with a party quest before..."

"Miss Milia, I never breathed a word saying that I'd help."

"Oh, right. Branch Managerrrr?"

"What're you yelling for?" Iris, who'd been giving instructions to another employee, looked annoyed.

Milia explained the situation.

Without even the slightest hesitation, Iris replied, "Fine by me. I see no problem with it."

*Hey, wait a second.*

"I'm sure Roland can handle something like that."

"I mean...I *can*, but..."

"That's right. You did defeat a *powerful* monster, after all."

That *powerful monster* was presently taking a catnap at my feet.

"It's not as though something like this is unprecedented. So can we count on you? …I'm sure everyone will feel a lot more comfortable with you going."

Whispers began to snake across the room.

"Why's the branch manager trust him so much?"

"Like I know."

"What was that about a *powerful* monster?"

"It's got to be the gray bear. He beat that thing on his own."

"Still, fighting solo's different from being in a party."

"Is Roland really that powerful?"

"He's the first person who's ever been hired since the branch manager started doing interviews. He's got to secretly be a former king's knight from the Order of Chivalry or something."

My colleagues were making all manner of baseless assumptions about me. Perhaps finding that amusing, Iris let slip a dignified giggle.

"Aren't you bored of paper pushing? I'd say our other people can handle things without you for now."

"…If that's an order as the branch manager, then I'll do it as an employee," I said.

"You will? Thanks. Then I'm counting on you."

"Hmm… The branch manager and Mr. Roland…seem unusually trusting of each other…" Milia cast a troubled look at Iris and me.

After joining Neal and the other two at the guild entrance, I departed.

"Nice to meet you. I'm Roland. I look forward to working with you."

The short-haired, spear-wielding man let out a sigh. "I can't believe they're saddling us with *guild staff*... I suppose I should be thankful to go on the quest at all... Hey, you better not drag us down, you hear?"

"Understood. I'll make sure not to get in anyone's way."

The cleric also gave me a once-over. "You didn't come empty-handed, did you?" he asked.

"I'm not fussy when it comes to my equipment," I replied.

I chose my weapon depending on the situation. Fixating on only one kind hurt your survival rate.

"You seriously didn't bring anything? You tryin' to make us look bad...?" the man with the spear snapped.

"I might be a healer, but...I don't like the idea of having to cast more than necessary," the cleric added.

From the looks on their faces, it was clear that those two thought of me as a huge deadweight.

Neal, however...

"Boss, I look forward to working with you! It is such an honor to be tackling a quest together!" The archer gave a deep bow of the head.

"Could you stop calling me *boss*?"

"What about master?"

"That's even worse."

Based on their interactions, the three had likely formed only a temporary party so that they could take on this quest. The spearman was the front line, while the other two formed the rear guard. I decided on a middle position. That way I could support the man in front while also protecting those behind me if the need arose.

"Let's head to Rason Village."

At the cleric's direction, our four-person party set out.

Curiously, Rason Village had seen an increase in what were previously rarely encountered monsters. Our job was to drive them back or slay them. During the trip, each of my party members spoke of their previous quest accomplishments. If I was to evaluate their strengths objectively, the spear wielder was an E rank. The cleric...was an F, and Neil was likely around an E-minus.

Neal's *actual* adventurer rank was D, and the other two were actually C rankers.

"So...what's our essential fourth man able to do, huh?" inquired the man with the spear.

"Yes, well... Let's just say that I'm average at everything. There's no need to worry. I won't get in your way."

"Oh, is that so?"

As we approached the village, I caught the scent of soot on the wind.

"We should hurry." I tried to urge everyone to go faster.

"What's the hurry for?" asked the man with the spear.

"Regardless, I'm supposed to be the leader, so *I* will give the orders," the cleric said while seeming ruffled.

"Boss, what's wrong?"

*Of course.*

"There's black smoke rising from the direction of the village," I said.

"You sure it's not just a bonfire?"

"AwooooooOOOOOOOOO!"

I heard the blaring howl of a monster.

Unsurprisingly, the other three froze up.

Ahead, we could see a large red beast. Its size and coloring had to make it a red wolf.

"AwwwwooooooOOOOOOOOO!"

"Wh-what's with that thing?!" The spear wielder spoke for the other two.

*Have they never seen a red wolf before?*

"Please remain calm."

I could've taken the lead and defeated it, but a *normal* guild employee would've done nothing of the sort. Also, this wasn't my adventure. It was theirs. I refrained from butting in.

"A red wolf is a large lupine-type monster. Its main characteristics are its full-bodied red coat, its high speed, and its offensive power."

So long as they kept cool heads, I was sure these three could handle it... Red wolves usually stalked lands farther to the south, however.

The cleric began to bark out some orders. "Advance guard, go engage with the enemy! Archer, fire at will and—"

"Y-you've gotta be kidding me! Like hell am I getting near that thing!"

"Huh? That's what you're supposed to do as the advance guard!"

This really wasn't the time for them to be arguing.

"...It seems to be drawing near."

After another howl, the red wolf began charging at us.

"Uh, ahHHHHHHHHHHHHHHHH?!"

The spear wielder had turned his back to the enemy. I grabbed his torso and jerked him around so that the fleeing man was forced to stand in front of me.

"I said to stay calm."

"A-are you kidding me?! I'm gonna get eaten! I'm gonna end up the only one dead and—"

*Smack*—I hit him on the head.

"Y'OUCH?!"

"If you keep that up, you really will end up dead."

"What did you say?!"

"Ready your spear and drop your hips. Look straight into your opponent's eyes."

"Wh-what—?"

"Just do it."

Half in tears, the man readied his pole arm and lowered his stance like I'd told him. Almost immediately, the red wolf's charge began to stall.

"Wooooo…!"

"Uh, uhhh… I—I just need to do this?"

"Good job, buddy. Don't break eye contact. The spearhead is always supposed to be facing down the opponent."

"G-g-got it."

When I glanced behind me, the cleric looked dumbfounded and seemed at a loss for what to do. While red wolves were known for their speed and strength, their hides weren't particularly tough. Any blade could easily pierce their flesh. This one undoubtedly realized that and was very cautious of the spear leveled right at it. Now it was just a matter of not letting the red wolf's speed get the better of us.

The beast's pace slowed from a sprint to a canter as it wavered on how best to attack. Before long, it had moved to a jog.

"Fire!" I shouted.

"L-leave it to me!"

Compared to the speed at which the killer falcon had been moving, this target was nothing. The pressure wasn't nearly as intense, either.

"Ngh."

Neal's arrow found purchase.

"Awooooo?!"

Even if it'd been farther, the red wolf's body was enormous. Hitting it after it'd charged so close to us was a trivial matter.

"One more!"

A second shaft pierced the beast's head, right above the nose.

"Graaawoooo?!"

The red wolf spasmed as it fell.

"Spear!" I instructed.

I'd been holding on to the man's belt to make sure he wouldn't try to run again, but now I released him and pushed him forward with a shove on the back.

"O-okay! I-I'm going! AhhhhhhHHHHHHHH!" The man let loose a war cry as he thrust his weapon into the bear-size wolf.

"Graaauuu..."

What life remained in the red wolf was snuffed out.

The spear wielder flopped onto his behind, crying. "W-we're saved... If you hadn't been giving directions, I would've— I..."

"Not attacking also takes nerve. You did well."

"Th-thank you!"

I gave the spear wielder a couple of pats on the back in recognition of his hard work.

"That was my first time seeing a monster like that, but boss had it all under control... He's the real deal...," Neal muttered.

*Please stop calling me "boss."*

The cleric still seemed out of sorts and was having trouble grasping everything that'd happened.

"I'll give the orders going forward. Is that fine with you?" I asked.

"Oh, ha-ha, yes... P-please do...o-of course."

I urged the three along, and we hurried to the village. The closer we got, the more apparent it became that the place was in chaos. Hot wind assailed the skin, and the smell of soot grew strong.

"Boss, the entire place is burning!"

"Yes, it seems so."

While I hadn't bothered with polite phrasing during our first battle, I decided to speak more formally outside of combat. When we got to the village, we found its people drawing water from a well and working to extinguish the blaze. I'd been hoping to ask them what happened, but getting the fire under control took priority.

As we were helping with the firefighting...

"Hey, guild staffer, word is that the place is burning because of some monster attack."

The spear wielder had gone questioning the villagers for me.

"Is that so? That certainly explains things..."

"According to the villagers, it was a huge lizard-looking creature."

A fire-breathing reptilian creature almost certainly meant a salamandra. Much like the red wolf, however, I'd never heard of one in these parts. Both usually resided much farther south...

I wasn't going to be able to fight a salamandra and give orders to the others at the same time. This was a C-rank quest, but facing a salamandra was a task far above that level.

"All right. Please continue to combat the flames," I said.

"Yup, you got it."

As the three other party members helped with the firefighting, I took a look around the neighborhood and quickly discovered a set of large footprints.

"..."

Four toes. Each of them was long and spindly—its claws were massive. I even found the trail the thing's dragging tail had left in its wake. Tracks like these had almost certainly been made by a salamandra.

Judging by the path it'd left, not much time had passed since it started all the commotion. It couldn't have gone far. With the tracks as my guide, I gave pursuit.

A short way ahead, I spotted a monster kicking up a cloud of dust as it moved.

"Found you."

Upon my making my murderous presence known, the salamandra jolted to a stop.

"Cree...?"

Immediately, the creature rose to its hind legs and had a glance around. This action meant that it was on alert. Curiously, it didn't seem entirely wild.

"Was this monster in captivity…?"

I tried to get closer, but the salamandra saw me.

"Creeeeeee!" It attempted to menace me by raising a shrill cry.

It was admirable for the creature to try and frighten me off, though I suppose it could also have simply been because the salamandra was a fool with no sense of its opponent's abilities. If the latter really was the case, I wasn't even going to need my skill.

There was a sharp rush of air as the salamandra inhaled.

"Greeeeeeeeee!"

A jet of flame erupted from its mouth.

The fire surged toward me with a deafening roar. I extinguished it with a single motion of my arm.

"Gweh…??" The salamandra cocked its head to the side. "Greeeeeeeeee!"

Again, it breathed fire. Evidently, this was its go-to attack. This time, it swept the flames from right to left, as though trying to scorch all around it.

Attempting to dodge a maneuver like that seemed idiotic, so I just let it come.

"Gweh…?"

Unable to understand what was happening, the lizard-like creature cocked its head to the side once more.

"As long as I move faster than the flames can keep up, I won't get burned."

"Greeeeeeeeee!"

The salamandra got on all fours and charged me.

"You're getting your just deserts for making a mess out of that village."

"GreeeeeeEEE!"

Once the salamandra was close enough, it reared up on its hind legs again and prepared to slash at me with its long talons.

At that same moment…

I plucked one of the creature's hands off its wrist.

"…Gweeeeeeeh?!"

Turning the monster's own razor-sharp claws on itself, I thrust them into the salamandra's throat.

"GreeeeeeEEEH!"

*Thud!* I whacked my enemy's forehead for good measure; then I granted the convulsing salamandra a release from its suffering.

"Sorry. I came empty-handed, so I had to use them. You had some good claws."

Having breathed its last, the salamandra let its cry warble into silence.

Feeling a sudden gaze on me, I whirled to stare into a dense thicket.

"…"

Before dealing with this new presence, I decided to head back to the village and tell everyone about the salamandra.

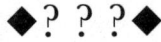

*H-he defeated the salamandra so quickly…! Not to mention that he somehow extinguished its flames with only his arm.*

Even though I had been observing from a decent distance, I had seen enough to know how things had ended.

*Whoa...! Th-this guy's dangerous!*

He didn't look much like an adventurer, but he had to have been around rank A, just like I was. Perhaps even higher...

Pondering such things didn't matter much now, though.

I'd never seen something so crazy before.

"—Hmm? ...Is he looking at me?"

*No way.*

There had to have been a good half mile between us.

*There's no way...*

"..."

In all my life, I'd never encountered someone so needlessly strong. Describing him as just *strong* didn't even do it justice. This guy was on a completely different level. No, a different dimension.

He hadn't raised a finger against the red wolf...but this cinched it.

I grabbed the salamandra's tail and dragged it back to the village.

Upon my return, I was pleased to find that the fires had all been put out. Everyone looked exhausted.

"Oh, boss man! Where'd you wander off to?"

I pointed at the salamandra I had left at the edge of the settlement.

"I was hunting down that thing. It's the one that set the village on fire."

"Whoaaa! That's one big lizard! Did you beat it yourself, boss?!"

"Crap, if this thing jumped out at me, I'd have wet myself..."

"I would've run away for sure…"

The three of my party members looked the salamandra up and down with great curiosity.

"Are you the leader?" a middle-aged man called to me. I nodded in the affirmative.

"Yes. My name is Roland. We came to this village on a quest… Anyway, I'm just glad that you were able to get the fire under control."

"Ah, a quest… I am the head of this little town. We owe you a great deal."

"Not at all. I simply defeated the monster that attacked you. If you could, please have a look and confirm it's the creature that started the fire. That's it over there." I pointed in the direction of the salamandra. The other members of the party were still examining it.

"Ah, yes, that's it; that's the one…! That giant lizard and crimson-colored wolf were the ones that attacked the village."

"Rest assured they won't be troubling you any further. Were they the monsters listed in the quest?"

The village leader nodded again.

"Yes, I believe they came about once a week…"

"I see… I am very sorry that we were so slow in dealing with this."

The man shook his head several times.

"I heard that you defeated the wolf on your way here. You're our saviors."

Neal and the other two had been listening to the exchange and did not look entirely displeased. I could empathize with them there. Receiving thanks for solving a problem like this was a good feeling.

"Thank you," the village leader said, bowing his head as he took my hand.

As I had a look around, the village leader filled me in on recent events.

"Everyone's been terrified, thinking we were going to be dealing with those monsters forever. People were careful, but we still suffered some losses."

There were burned houses every which way you looked. Some had been reduced to little more than charcoal. I could still feel residual heat radiating from them. I also spied a number of vacant domiciles. Many had no doubt abandoned the village. Corpses sported bite marks that matched the jawline of the red wolf. Evidently, the two monsters had been assigned roles.

The red wolf attacked the people, while the salamandra destroyed buildings.

"Before the monsters came, Rason Village used to be a peaceful little place. It was a normal sort of settlement you could find almost anywhere," the village leader explained.

"It certainly isn't a very large village," I observed.

"Yes... I understand why so many fled."

"I'm sure living in fear of being attacked becoming something *normal* would be difficult to endure."

"You're right... Was that crimson-colored wolf...a greater monster? Do you think of it as a high-ranking sort of creature?"

"The red wolf? They're known to be intelligent, though that can vary a bit. There are some that can even follow orders."

"I see." The village leader's face went somewhat dark. "Do you know of a humanoid monster that looks a bit like a pig? ...I suppose you'd call them orcs."

"I do. What of them?"

"When we were attacked, that great wolf would carry a group

of them in with it. They destroyed our fields, violated our women, and killed any men who stood against them… It was a terrible affair. Unsurprisingly, many departed from our village after that…"

"…"

*That look in his eyes…*

"…You were all living *normal lives*, weren't you?" I asked.

"Yes. It was a simple existence, but we had the sort of average lives I imagine most do."

*I see…*

At one time, these people had possessed the *normal life* I yearned for.

"Things should be safe now, sir. The monsters won't trouble you any further, and you should be able to return to how things used to be. Those who left may even hear about this and come back," I said.

"Yes, of course. Please let me thank you again."

"There's no need. You've made your gratitude quite clear already… Incidentally, that salamandra's hide is tough, but if you skin it, the meat is rather good. What do you think of that?"

The village leader grinned.

"That sounds very good. After all the terror it gave us, it seems only right to eat it."

The villagers began to prepare a small, celebratory banquet. The main dish was comprised of various cuts of the salamandra that I had sectioned myself. The thigh meat, enjoyed by the children and adults, was the most popular. The liver, heart, diaphragm, and other internal organs, while not looking very appetizing, were popular with the adults. After everyone enjoyed their meals, many villagers came over to where the party was sitting and offered their gratitude.

I'm not sure how to explain it, but this atmosphere felt similar to Milia's house.

...*Oh, that's right*... I remembered. This feeling...was *warmth*.

The people of Rason Village were very kind.

"We're being treated like heroes, boss," Neal said.

"It's an indication of how terribly this village was suffering," I replied.

"I'm real glad that I followed your instructions back with the wolf, guild staffer. If it wasn't for you, I'd be..." The spear-wielding man trailed off.

"Yeah... I wasn't able to do much, but...the people look so happy. Staffer, I'm going to work even harder," promised the cleric.

Each one of them eagerly sunk their teeth into the meat and partook of the drink that had been provided to them. The quality of the spirits wasn't great, but it hardly mattered when among such gracious and joyous people.

It reminded me of a time when I was still with Almelia's party. We'd liberated a town that had fallen into the hands of the demon lord army and received a similarly warm reception.

"Itz awll thanks to youuu. Like, serisly, um, thanks...you." The village leader was staggering toward us. He seemed pretty drunk.

He wrapped his arms around Neal, the spear wielder, and then the cleric.

Curious about something, I stood from my seat. I'd detected that the same presence from earlier had now entered the village.

After stowing the glasses I'd been wearing, the warm feeling of the celebration began to dim, and a chill permeated my chest.

"I know you're here. Come out," I demanded.

"What is with you?! What are you? You *look* like a guild employee."

The person who'd been watching me finally made their appearance. He was a man with brown hair that went down to his shoulders. Both his ears sported several piercings. The armor he wore was first-class.

"Does it matter what I am?"

"You're no fun. I got a good look at your fight. You're more than some normal guy if you did in my salamandra and red wolf so easily." The adventurer cackled wickedly.

"I'd suspected that someone had been ordering those monsters around; I suppose that's you..."

"Yup, it was me, all right. Ah, that reminds me—I never told you my name."

"I don't care to know it."

I didn't want this conversation lasting longer than it needed to.

There was something I wanted to ascertain, however.

"You're so cold. Heh-heh-heh. I'm a monster tamer and an A-rank adventurer. Truth is, I've been looking for some powerful partners."

"And?"

"That salamandra and red wolf were weak, and I didn't need them anymore. I can just as easily find a newer, more powerful monster to tame... So since I'm looking for some strong companions, I thought of a plan for killing two birds with one stone."

"—That's quite enough. I believe I understand where you're going with this, so stop talking."

The man looked puzzled and then continued to speak as though he was relishing this. He was like a kid who'd found a new game to play. Without a shred of criminality, he explained his little scheme.

"If you attack a village, *some* adventurer is bound to show up, right? It's not like the Order of Chivalry or the private soldiers of any old aristocrat would come out to some nowhere settlement. So anyway, set things up so the adventurers who show will fight my monsters. If they're weaker than my pets, then there'd be no point in recruiting them, see?"

"…Do you have any idea what that attack did to this village?"

"No clue. But who really cares? Might as well blame it on the demon lord army's stragglers. I mean, look, I'm an A-rank adventurer, and I've saved tooons of people on tooons of quests. I can do a li'l harm once in a while, can't I?"

"…"

"Actually, this has been helping me power up, so it's not like those people died for nothing. This puny village is doing a great service."

"You robbed these villagers of the livelihoods they've been working hard to preserve. No one has the right to steal that *normalcy*."

"The weak are destined die. That's all there is to it, right? Has peace boggled the ol' noggin with the war ending? C'moooon."

"I can never forgive anyone who so callously robs another of their *normal life*."

The *normal* I knew was placid, precious, and warm.
I knew exactly how difficult it was to obtain that.
"You won't forgive me, eh? Aight, aight, then what're you gonna do about it?"

"I'll kill you."

"Heh-heh-heh. Don't go assuming that's gonna be easy. I can still fight on my own—monsters or not."

"You talk big for a dead man."

"Huh? —Ghhhk?!"

Spitting up blood, the man took a few shaky steps. His eyes rolled back in his head as he collapsed. I fixed him with a glare as I watched him spasm on the ground. Just as I'd thought, he was a nobody. I hadn't even needed to use my skill on him.

"I evaluate your battle ability as a D."

The man hadn't even been able to follow my attack. It would've been one thing had I attacked from his blind spot, but I'd moved in on him head-on. He hadn't even known anything out of the ordinary had taken place.

*Is this the most an A-rank adventurer is capable of?*

"Such is your punishment for stealing and trampling on the normal lives of others."

Eventually, the man bled out and died.

I put my glasses on and headed back.

Many nocturnal monsters were drawn by the scent of human flesh and blood.

The man who had attacked the village was likely to be nothing but bones come morning.

During my return to the village, I heard boisterous voices, singing, and the occasional finger whistle.

"Boss…" Neal, who seemed to have been waiting for me, got on his knees and bowed his head. "P-please make me your disciple."

"No."

"Whaaa…? You decided way too quickly!"

"The village leader said he would lend us lodgings; we should take him up on it."

"Listen, um… After you left the party… I, er, got curious about where you went…"

"…"

"I—I didn't see or hear anything."

"Well then, please keep it that way."

I walked past Neal, who again lowered his head to me.

"I! I'm already thirty-three, but I'm still a low-rank adventurer with no hope of advancement. I started this life because I wanted to do something big, but I haven't been able to escape D rank…"

"Mr. Neal, even if I did teach you, all you'd learn from me are the fundamentals."

"I-I'll do anything! So please—"

"Best move inside before it gets too dark. You'll catch a cold."

With that, I headed to one of the beds the village leader had prepared at his house. I wondered what Rila was doing. So long as she was at the guild, Milia or another staffer would probably feed her. She was likely doing fine.


The next morning, our party departed from Rason Village, much to the disappointment of its people. Having stayed up all night drinking, the spear wielder and cleric bid their farewells with breath that reeked of alcohol. When we finally returned to Lahti, we stopped in at the Adventurers Guild to report on the quest status.

"Oh, Mr. Roland! Thank you for your work. How was it? How'd things turn out?" Milia, the one who'd been managing the quest, grinned as she helped us at the reception desk.

Behind her was a very sullen-looking black cat. It glared daggers at me throughout the entire conversation with Milia.

"There were no problems. Everyone was excellent," I reported.

"I see. I'm so glad," Milia said.

"That's not true!" the spear wielder cut in. "We did nothing but drag him down. We boasted about our abilities and were sure the mission would be a piece of cake. But as soon as a more powerful monster than we'd expected showed up, we all panicked…"

The cleric picked up from there. "That's right. The staffer was incredibly collected even when facing that unexpected enemy. Plus, his instructions were precise enough that we were able to defeat a red wolf without suffering any injuries."

"What?! A red wolf?! Y-you might have all been goners at your rank…!" Milia exclaimed.

"We owe our lives to the boss. Having him around is weirdly reassuring… Anyway, he looked way cooler during the fight than you ever would've expected. Reliable, too."

"Oh yes, I can certainly imagine. Mr. Roland doesn't look like it, but when things come down to the wire, you can really count on him!" Milia nodded with enthusiasm.

My three party members agreed, returning the gesture while saying, """That's for sure."""

As they spoke, Milia went through the procedures of completing the quest.

"Mr. Roland, you'll get a special bonus and reward for this when you're paid your salary."

"I will?"

"Yes, since accompanying people on quests comes with dangers, you'll receive extra compensation. It depends on the rank of the quest you go on, but you also get the next day off. That means you've got no work today."

"You mean to say that after doing something as *simple* as that, I get the next day off as a bonus?"

""""It wasn't *simple*,"""" everyone else said at once.

I still just really did not understand how they evaluated how strong monsters were in this Adventurers Guild. Then again, lately, I had seen quest ranks along with the monsters targeted for slaying and more or less had an idea of what was standard.

"What was so *simple* about that, boss? There was even a salamandra. A red wolf and a salamandra... For a party at our rank, it would've taken a whole week to come up with a counterplan to bring them down," Neal said.

"A-a-a salamandra??? What? No one told me anything about that," Milia said.

The spear wielder and cleric filled her in on the various details.

"If we'd known a monster like that was involved, we would've needed to increase the quest rank a lot more. A-and yet, you still did it! No one would've sent you on the quest had we known something that strong was waiting for you, Mr. Roland. Plus...I'd be worried sick..."

During my training in the mountains, I had become familiar with various flora and fauna to some extent. Furthermore, I'd faced a great many monsters during the war.

My experience with so many different kinds of opponents beyond demons gave me a natural handle on their traits and behavioral patterns. That knowledge had made the red wolf and salamandra fairly simple opponents.

"Milia, were you really that worried about us...?"

"You're such a nice person, Milia."

"Oh, no. I was only worried about Mr. Roland."

""Of course...,"" the spear wielder and cleric muttered in unison.

I left the rest of the reporting procedure to my party and Milia and went to the branch manager's office. As I knocked, I could hear a voice telling me to enter.

"Pardon the intrusion," I said, shutting the door behind me.

"Welcome back. Milia is so loud, I've already heard most of what happened. Seems like you kept busy."

Iris gestured to a sofa, and I sat myself down. Then I began to recount the events of the excursion.

"I see... So it was an A-rank monster-tamer adventurer... Unforgivable."

"I don't understand how the ranking system works, but according to Milia's reaction, it seemed like the quest should've been higher."

"When someone makes a request to our Adventurers Guild, they must prepare a handling fee and reward according to the rank. Given the village's distress...C rank might've been the best they could do."

Thinking back, I remembered that the quest slip hadn't detailed the particulars of the monsters that'd been assailing Rason Village. They hadn't lied, but they hadn't exactly told the truth, either.

"They did have extenuating circumstances when it came to that. Though it also is our job to decide on the rank..."

Iris's brow furrowed as she appeared to consider something troubling.

"Oh, also, what happened to that egotistical tamer? The one who had the monsters attack the village?"

"His whereabouts are unknown."

After thinking for a bit, Iris smiled slightly.

"...Ha-ha, is that so? There indeed are many cases of adventurers going missing." After writing something on a document, she stopped and looked back up. "This isn't in thanks for what you did, but...don't you have the day off? How does dinner sound?"

"No, I can't today."

"M-my treat."

"That isn't the issue."

"I don't mean the taverns around here. We'd go to an elegant luxury restaurant."

"I'm sorry—I need to take care of my cat."

"I-I've lost to a cat...! Usually when I extend an invitation, men immediately accept..."

"Uh-huh..."

"Fine. Hurry up and get out of here. Go home and rest."

Iris snapped a quill she was holding and chased me out of the room.

As I walked down the hall, I thought over what I would do with the sudden, unexpected day off I had been given.

*Mroooowl!*

The cry of a tiny animal caught my attention. Looking down, I spotted a black cat with its fur standing on end.

"What a lovely night you must have had leaving me behind! I heard it all! Enjoy your banquet?! I was chased mercilessly by that wench Milia and was forced to eat tasteless cat food…! I'm practically balding from the stress."

"Sorry. Let's buy something on the way home."

"Hmph… Meat and ale, then. I will accept nothing less."

"Got it."

I left the guild and perused a few shops that were only just opening their doors. Once I had what I needed, I made the trek back to my house on the outskirts of town.

I ended up spending a good amount on food and drink in order to appease the demon lord. I was supposed to be getting some kind of bonus, though, so money probably wasn't going to pose an issue.

After returning Rila to her original form, we ate and drank for a good while. Sitting side by side on a sofa, I told her about a few different things from my trip.

"That might have been my first time killing someone of my own accord."

"You're surprisingly sensitive to such things. How was it? How did it feel to kill someone of your own choosing? Did knowing it hadn't been a command make things different?"

"Nothing quite so dramatic, but I'd like to avoid it going forward, if at all possible."

"What a naive thing to say; you are as innocent as a maiden. Ha-ha-ha." Rila gave a low chuckle as she swirled a glass of wine. It wasn't even the afternoon yet, but Rila downed it like it was juice. "I cannot help but consider it strange that this is the man who defeated the demon lord, once hailed as the strongest of all time."

I wondered why I'd brought up my feelings on killing at all. It wasn't as though I was drunk.

"I never thought I'd care this much about it," I admitted.

"It has nearly been a month since you defeated the demon lord and have been leading a *normal life*... Have you changed your mind—or perhaps have you begun to separate your identity as an assassin from your identity as Roland?"

"That might be it."

Confidentiality naturally went hand in hand with assassination. While that hadn't been the only reason, I had gone out of my way to avoid making personal connections in the past.

Ever since I had begun to make my own way as an assassin, I had felt isolated.

"Serving as the demon lord was solitary in its own way as well. Final decisions and responsibility were constantly sought from me. I could not exist as Rila; I always had to be 'the demon lord.' I may be the only one in this world able to understand your solitude."

The words of the demon lord were a killing blow of sorts.

Though the nature of a king's solitude and that of an assassin's might've been different, it was certain that they were both a kind of loneliness. Perhaps that's why I'd confided in Rila.

When I put my arm around Rila's hips, she put hers around my neck. We hugged each other close and shared a long, drawn-out kiss.

"Rila, when I'm with you, I feel an odd sense of *warmth*," I confessed.

Rila blinked several times, then her cheeks went red.

"I-i-is that so? I—I am pleased...... Um, I...um, well... I also... feel *warmth*...when I am with you..."

For some reason, she fidgeted as she whispered her reply.

She wouldn't look at me at all and was even covering her face with her hands.

# 9

# The Famed Guild Staffer

"Welcome. How can I help you today?"

After several weeks of nothing but document filing, my work finally started to gravitate more toward reception-desk duties. Putting aside whether that was *normal*, it had become routine for me.

"Uh, um, you're Mr. Argan, right?"

"…Yes, I am."

That was what it said on my name tag. I occasionally forgot the name, however, and was forced to check the little pin myself.

"Oh, no, I was just making sure. Sorry." The adventurer nervously waved his hands at me.

Was there something special about me helping him?

"I heard a lot about you from my mentor, Neal."

"Neal spoke of me?"

"Yes, he said that I can't go wrong accepting any quest you recommend."

"Please don't take what others say as fact, sir."

Continuing to make light conversation, I looked over the adventurer's permit and assigned him a suitable quest.

"There are rumors that the quests you recommend have low injury rates."

*Ah, so that's the reason.*

I had memorized much of the surrounding geography, as well as its various inhabitants.

For slaying quests, I'd suggest things like what necessities to pack, information on the target, any good areas to rest, and escape routes. For the most part, the adventurers would report back with no injuries.

Over time, I came to find that I enjoyed hearing adventurers talk excitedly about their excursions. I even thought it was fun.

Someone calling Neal their mentor was a surprise, however. Perhaps because he was older than the young adventurer I was currently helping, he appeared to be more experienced.

"Please pick out a quest that looks right for me."

"Very well."

While described as "low injury rates," it was actually more like "success rates," since those injured too seriously ended up dead and never returning. No one wanted that, so every adventurer paid careful attention to the various injury rates that quests carried with them.

"I'd really like to avoid any nasty wounds. Won't be able to make money otherwise," said the adventurer I was helping.

"I know that very well," I answered.

If recovery took two months, that meant two months with no income. That much was true of any job but perhaps even more so when it came to adventuring work in particular.

The adventurer, who seemed to have taken a liking to the slaying quest I had chosen, quickly went on his way.

"Looks like you've gotten comfortable with the reception desk. I feel reassured when I see you there," Milia said from behind me.

"Miliaaa, I could do that, toooo. Piece of caaaake."

"Mr. Maurey, just how many years do you think you've worked this job? You've been here for over a decade, haven't you? I'd be more concerned for you if it *wasn't* a piece of cake by now."

"...Hey, why are you so mean? ...I'm supposed to outrank you, you know...?"

"It's only been a month since Mr. Roland started working here. Sometimes he blurts out odd things, but his work is flawless, and he has a very good reputation."

"Come on, now—don't make me laugh, Milia. Heh-heh, I've got a pretty good reputation among adventurers myself, you know."

"The only ones you have a good reputation with are those you're friends with, right?"

"...Quit chattering and do your job... Milia, my girl, you've got to keep your hands busy. No stopping."

"...Hmph."

When I called the next adventurer over, a boorish-looking, short-haired young man approached. He plunked himself down into the seat and placed his feet on the counter.

"I'm countin' on you for a sweet quest."

"Very well."

I spied Neal in the back of the room.

"According to your rank, you are eligible only for F-rank quests. There are no monster-slaying quests today, but we do have herb-collection and delivery quests. Which would you prefer?"

"Hunh?" The young man scowled at me. "Which would I prefer? What're you talkin' about? Bring out the big quests. I know you got 'em."

"I'm afraid you are an F-rank adventurer, so these are the only appropriate quests I may prepare for you. Thank you for your understanding."

"Hunnnh? You're lookin' at an adventurer, you know? You can't exist without us, you know?"

"I'm afraid that is a separate matter."

"Quit your nitpicking!"

When he saw the commotion, Neal the adventurer quickly came over.

*Slap!* He hit the young adventurer on the head.

"Ow?! S-sir?!"

"You better not be making trouble for the staff!"

"I-I'm sorry!"

Neal's gaze turned to me as if to ask, *Isn't that right?*

"You better get your feet off the counter, you little punk!"

"Y-yessirrr!"

Neal's gaze turned to me as if to ask, *Isn't that right?*

"Without guild staffers, we wouldn't even have quests to go on, you know. You got that? Don't go getting full of yourself, F rank!"

Neal's gaze turned to me as if to ask, *Isn't that right?*

I just couldn't help but feel fed up with Neal's annoying stares.

"Y-you're completely right! I'm really sorry!"

"What's apologizing to me gonna do?"

"Sorryyyyyy!"

The tough attitude the younger adventurer had been exhibiting was entirely gone now. He bowed his head in my direction.

"My apologies…," he said.

"That's it?! You better say, *I deeply apologize for the inconvenience I caused*!"

"I—I deeply apologize for the inconvenience I caused!"

Neal forced the kid's head down even lower.

"I'm sorry for my mentee, boss. I recognize him from the neighborhood, so I'll make sure to give him a good, long talking-to," Neal proclaimed.

"B-boss…?" When the adventurer glanced at me, his eyes went wide. "What?! Is he the boss you're always talking about, sir?! The one who got a four-person party to the point that they could beat a red wolf…?! I-I-I've heard about that saga so many times! It's the entire reason I wanted to become an adventurer! I heard everybody would've died if you hadn't been there, boss. I always thought you were supercool…"

"You haven't got the right to call him 'boss'!" Neal exclaimed.

Actually, I had no recollection of saying it was fine for anyone to call me "boss."

"Come to think of it, what're you doing sitting down?! Get to your feet! C'mon! Acting like you're on the boss's level, are you?!"

"I-I'm sorry!"

Truthfully, it was easier for me if the adventurer sat back down.

When I started to explain the quest, the adventurer was half standing with his hands on his knees as he nodded in agreement.

"I got it! You can count on me!"

"Boss, he's a doofus, but I hope you'll look after him anyway."

Neal gave a mechanical sort of bow, and the younger adventurer mimicked the motion.

"Well then, I'll excuse myself."

"P-pardon me."

Remembering something, I called out, "Mr. Neal."

"Yes, sir?"

"Congratulations on rising to rank C."

He had completed a quest I had arranged for him a few days ago and had consequently risen a rank. I hadn't been the one to receive that report, so I'd missed my chance to congratulate him.

"Thank you so much! I owe it all to you, boss…! I hope we can continue to work together!"

"Same to you."

After one last bow, Neal and his mentee left.

When the time came, I switched places at the reception desk with Milia. No sooner had I done so than Iris called me over.

"It seems that the adventurers you've been managing have been getting stronger lately."

"I've been handing them quests that require slightly more than what they're usually capable of, so I think that gives them courage."

Courage was pretty much the same thing as spirit. If they were successful, that tied in to their confidence. If they continued to succeed, that would turn into competence.

"It's hard enough to ascertain an adventurer's abilities, but you're assigning them things beyond their current limits? Won't they fail if even the tiniest thing goes wrong?"

"Yes, it's exactly as you say. That's why I also give them advice."

"Hmm, how very like you."

With an elegant smile, Iris sauntered out of the building.

The staff was practically in an uproar.

"She actually praised an employee…?!"

"I thought the branch manager was afflicted with a case of no-praise-for-anybodyitis this entire time..."

"But she's always so cold to us..."

"The only one she fawns over is the new guy. Roland, right? Isn't that kinda unfair? Why is that?"

I spent the rest of the day filing documents.

Around closing time, Milia, having inched her way over to my desk, sneakily left me a letter.

*Do you have time today? Would you like to eat somewhere?*

I thought for a bit, then wrote back, *I'm sorry. Today is a little inconvenient.*

Upon receiving my reply, Milia groaned. "Ughhh..."

"Roland, what do you think of doing something today?" Iris asked, catching me on my walk home.

"I'm sorry, but I need to take care of my cat."

"Grrr... That cat again...!"

Rila hadn't come to my workplace today.

"You've sure got some nerve turning down an invitation from your superior...! Oh, right, right, it's actually about a work-related matter, so what do you think about doing it at an elegant and luxurious place I have a reservation at? Over drinks?"

"If it's regarding work, please speak to me about it during business hours. If you'll excuse me..."

"Grrr... He's so strangely straitlaced...!"

Dodging a trembling Iris, I resumed my trip home.

Rila was waiting for me at the house. Perhaps she'd found herself with too much time on her hands, because she'd recently become rather obsessed with cooking. Since I didn't care how anything tasted, I thought pretty much whatever I ate was fine. That had put her in a good mood, so she had taken to making and bringing me dinner every day.

Upon my arrival, I found Rila at the entrance to the house, wearing a self-satisfied smirk.

"Ha-ha-ha-ha! Listen well, knave! For I am proud of my supper today!"

Rila closed her eyes expectantly, so I gave her a kiss on the lips. Sometimes that alone wasn't enough, but today it seemed a quick peck sufficed.

We sat down for dinner and partook of the veritable mountain of food that had been stacked on the dining table.

Once that was done, I planned to take a bath and go to bed. Occasionally, I'd also have sex with Rila. When morning arrived, I'd need to get up and go back to work.

Such was how I was spending my recent—though maybe not *normal*—days.

# 10

# The Roadside Girl

I was on my way home after grocery shopping for a few things Rila had asked for.

The people around town had been afraid of Rila at first, but once they figured out she meant no harm, fewer and fewer of them took issue with her. When she came by my workplace, she would usually change into her cat form to avoid complications, but when I wasn't around, she would go out shopping freely in her original form. She seemed to enjoy wandering around town.

When I passed through an alley that was a shortcut, I sensed a presence that made me pause.

"…"

I peered into a hiding place and found a child. A petite ten-year-old girl, to be exact.

She was curled up and hugging her knees.

"What are you doing in a place like this?" I asked.

Her clothes barely amounted to so much as rags. It didn't take much to guess what this child was.

She didn't answer even after I waited for some time.

The sight of her brought to mind a certain memory.

"Are you hungry?"

I offered the girl some of the bread Rila had tasked me with buying. At that point, her empty eyes looked up at me as though actually noticing me for the first time. There was a brand of servitude on her neck, just as I had expected. No doubt she was a slave who'd either escaped or been abandoned.

"Eat," I said, as though an order. Slowly, the girl began to nibble at the bread. Her pace steadily quickened.

Once she was done, she turned her face away from me again.

"Were you abandoned?" I asked.

The girl remained silent and unresponsive.

Maybe she had run away.

"Come with me. I'll look after you for a while."

"…"

Still, she refused to move…

Thinking that, perhaps, she was unable to move, I put my hands under her armpits, stood her up, and got her on my back so that I could carry her. I wondered if maybe she'd grown too weak because she hadn't been eating enough. My hope was that she would start talking again once she had her strength back.

"…That's how I ended up taking her home with me."

When I explained the situation to Rila after returning home with the groceries, she snorted at me.

"I'm going to look after her for a while."

"And why would you do something as wearisome as that? It is not as though anyone asked you to."

"…We have extra rooms, so I doubt it'll be inconvenient."

"Do as you please, I suppose."

While Rila was making dinner, I bathed the girl and dressed her in clothes that were too big for her.

After noticing that she was rubbing the sleep from her eyes, a possible result of the bath, I tucked her into bed in one of the spare rooms.

"Rila, is there a way to remove a brand of servitude?"

"Such methods do exist. However, I no longer possess mana, nor can I use magic."

"I know."

A brand of servitude is a crest that is stamped into slaves. A slaver casts a magic contract that forces the branded person into absolute obedience and prevents them from doing harm to their controller. The slave would then be sold off to a buyer.

"I doubt a grubby child such as that would fetch a high sum."

"I agree. She did clean up nicely after a bath, though."

The girl might've been an underservant for a merchant somewhere nearby. Aristocrats were not the sole buyers of slaves. The rich often only bought slaves for labor. That meant they would purchase primarily young men. This was a girl, however, which meant she might have been sold to someone looking to sate a particular penchant.

"Anyway, she likely either was abandoned or ran away."

"You are kind. Kind to the point that you almost seem as though you never were an assassin… So be it. I cannot guarantee the brand will be undone."

The brand of servitude and contract could be undone only by

the contract magic of the slaver who'd made it. If brands could be removed through purification magic, the slave trade wouldn't exist. That was why contract magic couldn't be manipulated except by its caster.

"To my knowledge, nothing can be done to remove the mark—but that only applies to the human magic that I know of," I said.

"Ha-ha, you are a crafty man."

Humans feared demons, but not simply because of their great quantity of mana or magical sensibilities. Demons were reviled because they possessed a number of magical arts beyond human understanding.

Rila went to the girl's room to check on the brand of servitude.

"...Hmm. There are several types of magic that a human could use for a slaving contract... This girl's mark, however, is a variety of common fiend contract."

"A fiend contract?"

"Hmm. It seems to be the type of agreement in which one receives an exorbitant amount of power in exchange for their soul. While that's what it appears to be, it also seems to have been tampered with."

Rila had divined all that just by glancing at the mark on the sleeping child.

"It has an irreversible structure... Humans truly can be far more terrifying than demons at times. The larger issue is whether you can actually handle the magic I know."

"May as well try. Teach me."

"Then I shall give you a personal lesson, direct from the demon lord herself. You should be grateful for my benevolence."

"You're not the demon lord anymore, though."

At my request, Rila taught me the theory and methodology of

the spell I would need, as well as the amount of mana it would take and the details of how to use that mana.

Her lecture was unexpectedly careful and gentle.

"I doubt a human such as you could do it…"

It'd been a number of years since I'd used magic that someone else had taught me.

I did exactly as Rila had instructed.

*"Dispell."*

"Oh! I nearly forgot! I am able to do this without a magic circle. You, however, must inscribe one or your success will—"

*Crack!*

There was a loud sound like shattering glass.

"Y-you were successful…"

"Is that it?"

The brand of servitude on the girl's neck was gone.

"All right. We'll ask her what happened when she wakes up tomorrow," I decided.

"Inconceivable. Dispell is court-order-rank penta purification magic… To think a human such as yourself would be successful on his first try. And without a magic circle, at that."

"Court-order-rank what?"

"Ah, yes. Demons have ranks just as humans do—according to our talents. The higher the court order, the stronger and more varied kinds of magic one may use. Court-order-rank mono indicates the types of magic only I, as the demon lord, may use."

Though there were exceptions, it seemed the court order was generally a good barometer for the power of most magic.

"I just did what you told me to, Rila."

"There are likely fewer than a hundred demons who could successfully cast Dispell after drawing a magic circle... Only a handful are able to do so without a magic circle, myself included."

"Really?"

"Hmm. It seems your abilities are not limited to the art of assassination. You can successfully cast something you have just learned from another on your first try. I have witnessed it myself. You stand out among the rest as having high magical talent. Perhaps even at the same level as a demon."

My magic had received the approval of the demon lord herself.

The next day, when I went to check on the girl, she was already out of bed.

Her color looked better than yesterday, too.

"Did you get a good night's rest?"

"..."

Like a cautious kitten, she stared me down.

I showed her both my palms and nodded several times.

"I'm Roland. I'm an assa—an Adventurers Guild employee. What's your name?"

"...Name...? Name...?"

"Do you not know?"

The girl squeezed her eyes shut as though she was slightly troubled and shook her head.

"Don't know."

Circumstances varied, but it wasn't unheard of for someone to be sold into slavery without ever being given a name. It was common among the children of prostitutes. Clearly, the poor girl was still very confused. It didn't seem likely she was going to explain everything in one go.

For the time being, I brought the breakfast Rila had made to our guest's room.

"I can't guarantee it'll taste good, but it's probably better than nothing."

"What was that smart remark I just heard?"

Rila was glaring at me from behind.

Luckily, the girl seemed to take to the food, eagerly sipping at the breakfast with her spoon.

*She must be traumatized…*

"Hmm? Is something the matter, knave…? You've been staring at me. Huh?! W-we cannot! Y-you cannot take me in your arms in front of such a young child! No, unacceptable…!"

Despite her protests, Rila looked slightly expectant.

As Rila clutched her chest and blushed, I touched her collar and turned her into a cat.

After she had transformed, she plopped onto the ground.

"Wha—?! I'm a cat now…? Knave, what is the meaning of this sudden development?"

"Kitty," the girl muttered.

I'd heard that caring for an animal helped people recover from trauma.

I grabbed Rila's collar.

"What are you doing?! Why have you made me transform?! Knave, are you listening to me?!"

Rila struggled as she kicked her feet back and forth.

The girl's eyes were glittering.

"A talking kitty…!"

"That's right. It's a talking kitty. Could you take care of this cat for me?"

"Excuse me—what was that?! Hurry and return me to my form! I said change me back! Right now!"

I handed a struggling Rila to the girl, who wrapped the cat in a tight hug.

"Kitty, you're warm."

"Gaaah?! My bones! You'll break them! Ease off! Please! Do you even know who I am?! This is blasphemy!"

It certainly was a very noisy little black cat.

"Is taking care of her…your order…master?"

"I'm not your master. If you don't want to do it, you don't have to… I'm heading off to work. If you need to know anything, ask the cat."

"Knave, I will have my revenge for this!"

I wasn't sure whether the girl had really heard what I'd said, but she took to playing with Rila rather quickly.

She hadn't been very interested in Rila's original form or me, though.

Cats were not to be underestimated.


I headed to the guild and began my workday.

I didn't intend on raising the kid. Taking care of her was just temporary.

*…What do I need to do to help the kid make her own way?*

"Hmm, right, the name registry—"

I pulled the adventurer name registry from the shelf. I looked through the list of adventurers who were registered to the guild.

"Seems we don't really ask for demographic information or age."

In order to register as an adventurer, one needed to pass a test. The only condition for taking it was that the applicant couldn't have been convicted of any serious crime.

"All right, in that case…"

I'd made my decision.

*HRMAAAOOOW!* Something like the cry of an animal echoed throughout the rooms.

"Kitty, shhh, shhh. Is this really it?"

"Mrwagh, mrwagh."

Everyone in the office turned to the door where the sound had come from. *It can't be*, I thought. I approached the door and opened it.

"Oh."

*Mrow.*

A black cat, clutched to a young girl's chest, looked up at me and smirked. Rila had gone out and brought the girl here. I guess this was her revenge.

"Why are you here?" I asked.

"Kitty said to come…"

*…Hmph.*

When Rila saw my face cloud, she snickered under her breath.

"Huh? Isn't that your kitty, Mr. Roland? And a child? Why is that little kid here?" Milia spoke up, vocalizing the question on everyone's mind.

"Well, it's… I'm taking care of her for a while…and I asked her to keep an eye on the house, but it seems she's followed me. I'm sorry—I'll get her back home immediately."

In a surprising turn of events, all my coworkers hurried over.

"Roland, who's the kid? A family member?"

"Yes, something like that…," I answered.

"She must've felt lonely being home alone and came all the way here with her cat."

"That's gotta be it."

The male staffers fawned over the girl clutching the cat close to her.

Next came the whisperings from my female coworkers.

"He's taking care of one of his relative's kids."

"She must be sooo attached to him if she's come all this way for him."

"He scores high for being able to take care of a child."

"Mr. Argan is reliable and kind, so of course a kid would like him."

""""He sure is nice…""""

Amid all the guild staffers who found the whole thing heartwarming, there was one man who hadn't so much as left his desk.

"Hey now, this ain't a nursery. Hurry up and take her on home. Right, everyone?" Maurey called.

"""" """"
...

Everyone shot him a cold look.

"Am I wrong here? I'm sure I'm not, right? This is a business. It's no place for looking after kids."

Maurey's face made it clear that he thought himself in the right.

*Hmm.* I thought it was a pretty sound argument, too. That was why I was trying to get her to go home, but—

"Actually, can you even watch a kid while working? There's no way you can, right? You got a lot of nerve, considering you're the bottom rung of the ladder, rookie. You better not be shirking your duties. You can't multitask like that till you get to my level, right? You've gotta become a full-fledged, trained pro like me before you even attempt that. Plus, I hate kids and how fussy they are."

No one said anything, but everyone in the office stared daggers at Maurey.

"…What? What's the problem? More importantly, get back to work. Gotta keep those hands busy."

I didn't disagree with his opinion on principle, but Maurey's attitude wasn't winning him any favors. That better-than-thou attitude rubbed others the wrong way.

"What's wrong, everyone? Huh? A child?" Iris had come to see what all the commotion was. When she saw the child, her eyes blinked a few times in rapid succession.

"Oh, Branch Manager…" Milia explained things to Iris in my place.

"Hmph, so that's what's going on."

Maurey still hadn't quit complaining. "Branch Manager, this is an office. It's no place for childr—"

"Why not? As long as she doesn't get in the way," Iris decided.

"Roland barely even can get his work done, though," protested Maurey.

"As far as I can see, he's proven fairly capable."

"He goes home earlier than everyone else. How could he possibly be doing all his work?"

"He does that because he's efficient."

"But I've been pulling late nights staying in to finish—"

"That's just because you're inefficient."

Like a slug that had been sprinkled with salt, Maurey shrank smaller and smaller.

"…You really didn't…mince words there…"

He choked back tears.

The branch manager's decision had settled things; the girl was allowed to stay at the Adventurers Guild for today. That didn't mean she could just run around the office, of course. Iris instructed me to keep her in the reception room.

"Can I play with the kitty cat here?"

"Yes. I'll come check on you every once in a while. Make sure to behave."

I patted the girl on the head.

Rila, the instigator of this whole debacle, merely yawned at our feet. This was the end of my leisurely days. I'd taken on the responsibility of raising a young girl so she could become an adventurer and make her own way in the world.

As I headed home from work, Rila gave the girl, still unaware of her original identity, a new name.

"Maylee. In old demonic, it means 'the blue sky.'"

"Hmm. Then that's what we'll call you. Maylee, that's your name now."

"Maylee? I'm Maylee?"

"Yes, that's right."

As she looked at me with eyes as blue as the sky, I gave Maylee a pat on the head.

"Maylee!" she squealed happily.

"It seems she likes it," I observed.

"Ha-ha. Why, of course. My flair for names extends deeper than the seas and higher than the heavens."

I didn't really understand what Rila was trying to get at, but it seemed she was praising herself.

"I'm going to train you so you can survive on your own, Maylee," I said.

"What does that mean?" she asked.

"I'm going to make you an adventurer."

"Hmm, not a terrible notion," Rila commented.

I'd realized it only recently, but Rila seemed nearly incapable of direct praise. *Not terrible* was about as good as I was going to get.

"As the remover of her brand of servitude, you would do well taking responsibility for her, knave."

"...But on the other hand, I will also teach her what's *normal*."

"So...is that where I offer my insight, then?" Rila made the haughtiest face her black-cat form could muster.

"No, not really."

"......"

"I think I'll ask Milia to handle that."

At those words, Rila leaped at me and swiped with her claws. I caught her, ran mana through her collar, and returned her to her original form.

"I don't suppose I know what normal is anyway," Rila admitted. Moody, she turned her face away from me.

The next day, I woke Maylee up before sunrise and began our training regimen. Our practicing continued when I returned home from work. Day in and day out.

"You were a slave, right?" I asked.

"Slay-vuh? No, my name is Maylee!"

"Well, that's not really what I meant."

We were on an early-morning jog through the mountains. Rather than taking the flat and level roads, we ran around the craggy paths and game trails. Her legs, which had been frail the first week we'd started, had rapidly gotten stronger. Kids certainly grew fast. Maylee, who claimed running was fun, was full of spirit from start to finish.

"You should do well to remember I am no housemaid," Rila spat.

"Would you like me to buy you a maid uniform?"

"No," she replied as she heated soup and prepared bread on the table after Maylee and I returned from our daybreak training session.

I suppose Maylee must have been used to eating pretty terrible food, since she never complained about Rila's cooking.

"I don't think of you as a housemaid."

"Then I am satisfied... Lately, all you've been doing is taking care of Maylee... Um, and you have neglected cherishing me as often as you used to..." Rila's voice was a whisper. Once she'd said her piece, she skulked away, escaping to another room.

"Do you want to train or something?" I asked.

"How absurd! Of course not! Why would I need to do something like that?!"

Rila had peeked from the door, shouted at me, and then immediately fled.

Apparently, I'd gotten it wrong.

Maylee was a good listener and an even faster learner. When I was her age, I had already begun working as an assassin, so I decided to give her some practical training tomorrow.

That night, as I lay in bed considering tomorrow's regimen, I sensed something unusual.

"..."

...A "rat"?

I touched Rila's collar as she slept and turned her into a cat. I slipped out of bed, making sure not to wake Maylee, who was sound asleep between us.

When I went outside, I spotted a lone man walking in the moonlight. His features were androgynous, but he sported no other distinguishing traits. Based on his mien, he was likely—

That's when the man caught sight of me.

"I was expecting her to be alone, but it seems fate has not been kind to you, mister."

"I could say the same of you," I replied.

"I'd thought myself undetectable."

"Your abilities are third-rate... Can't even hide correctly, hmm?"

"What did you say?"

"When you erase your presence, you're also erasing the presences of the things that surround you. It creates an unnatural void in the space around you. Where I should sense plants and trees, there's suddenly nothing. That fools no one. Unless you assimilate with your surroundings, all you do is draw attention."

"There's not a person alive who detects *absence*."

"I suppose it'd certainly seem that way to someone of your level."

"You sure are cocky for having merely run into me on your way home."

"You can't even tell that my coming outside was no coincidence?"

"Listen, assimilating with your surroundings isn't even possible."

"...That's what you think."

Doubtlessly, I didn't even need my skill to deal with this person, but I decided I'd show him some real strength. Taking in everything, the vegetation, the earth, the wind, the flowing stream, I melted into the scenery.

The man started following me with his eyes a moment too late—I'd already made my move. In that single moment, the entire fight was decided. I stole the man's concealed knife, and from behind, I wrapped my arm around his head such that the tip of his own knife was pointed at his eye.

"This is what the world is like. Do you understand now?"

"—Wha...? I can't...move... How—?"

"Looks like fortune wasn't on your side."

"...Kill me."

Despite my attempts to question the man, he refused to give up the identity of his target or his employer.

"I can't believe there's a creature in this world capable of seeing through my Absolute Ambush skill... You're repugnant. It's just as you say. I was unlucky..."

"Depending on the skill, it's something you fundamentally have to be discreet about invoking. How long does it take to invoke that whatever-it's-called skill of yours?"

"It doesn't matter. It'd be absolutely impossible to use my skill on an opponent like you..." The man gave a self-deprecating laugh. "I mean, this ended in two blinks of an eye. In just that short amount of time, you circled around me, found my hidden knife, and had it poised to strike... What's going on here...? Are you a pro?"

"No, I'm just an employee at the Adventurers Guild. Most of my days are spent pushing paper."

"Ah-ha-ha-ha. You liar. Considering the overwhelming difference in our abilities, all I can do is laugh. I always thought I'd die like a dog... Well, I suppose I should count myself lucky that my last breaths were spent facing an opponent like you..."

"This is a nice knife."

"Isn't it?"

Those were the man's last words.

Out of respect for his professionalism and refusal to leak any information, I gave him a quick death.

*...Did someone find out Rila is still alive? No, I sealed away the part of her that was the demon lord. If they were coming after Rila, I doubt they would've only sent a single assassin. In which case...*

◆

A few days had passed since I had defeated the mysterious assassin. Nothing out of the ordinary had occurred since.

"Roland, do you not have a name for that trick?"

Using a short tree branch as a dagger, Maylee was thrusting forward, accompanied by whooshing sounds.

"I don't."

We talked as I evaded Maylee's attacks. She seemed to have some amount of talent for fighting. Maylee was quickly absorbing everything I taught her. Whether it was how to carry herself or how to handle a weapon, she took to it easily. Just as dry sand took in water, the more I taught her about the rhythm of evasion, defense, and attack, the better she got.

"I think naming techniques is unnecessary, but you may give it a name if you like."

"Okay! Then this is the Back Slash!"

After deciding upon a name, Maylee charged around to my back. If she was to attack the way I'd taught her, she was liable to slash at me holding the tree-branch dagger with a backhand. Still facing forward, I firmly reached behind and grabbed Maylee's thin arm.

"Ah?! How?! You weren't even looking!" Maylee's face looked a lot less cheerful than it had been a moment ago.

"The name of your technique completely gives it away. Calling out something like that puts the opponent on their guard."

"B-but it's not cool if you keep quiet."

Dying trying to look cool didn't help anyone.

I thrust my pointer finger against Maylee's pale face.

"That makes two hundred and fifty-three times that you've died, Maylee."

The girl pouted and groaned as tears welled up in her eyes. "Grrrrrrrrrr... I hate you, Roland!"

Apparently, Maylee had gotten fed up with me not going easy on her. She threw the branch at me.

"Too easy." I flicked the stick away.

"Kittyyyyy! Roland's being meannnnn."

Maylee went running to Rila, who had spread out a sheet over the grass in order to watch the training.

"How many times must I tell you to call me Rila...? Maylee, this isn't a game. Roland knows what he's talking about."

Maylee squeezed Rila tightly in a hug. Rila, not seeming altogether displeased at that, hugged her back and stroked her hair.

"Roland is strong..."

"Indeed. He is the one and only being who was capable of defeating me. He wouldn't lose to a little urchin like you, Maylee."

"Nghhhhhhh." Maylee started to playfully hit Rila for not taking her side.

Rila broke into a laugh.

"However, knave, I do not believe an adventurer would need to know this technique."

"Though adventurers put their lives on the line, assassins risk even more. They require superior discipline when it comes to handling the trust of their employer, pressure, and the consequences of failure. If an adventurer screws up, they can merely run away and try again."

"Hmm," Rila answered. I couldn't tell whether she understood what I was getting at.

"Why not work on swordsmanship and hand-to-hand combat? Couldn't you teach her that?"

"I'm preparing her mind right now. Assassination techniques are methods that ensure a kill. An adventurer learns a few techniques with the expectation that they'll get by even if they fail. That is how they appear to an assassin. There is a great difference between those who believe there is a next time if they fail and those who do not."

"I see. So you're teaching her the art of assassination in order to cultivate her mentally, then?"

"Yes. Since maneuvers that ensure a kill are also maneuvers that ensure survival."

"That's quite persuasive, given you're the one saying it."

Maylee looked between Rila and me, trying to understand what we were talking about.

"However, I do believe in the time I haven't been watching, Maylee has become quite agile. That Back Slash from earlier did not have much force behind it, but it was a nimble and good strike."

"That's because Roland taught me…and gave me lots of advice…"

"While he is an ornery man, you would not be able to find anyone who could compare in the arts of battle even if you scoured the world." Rila sipped the tea she'd brought with her. "Don't you think that's about enough for now? Objectively, she seems more than capable."

"To me, she still has a long way to go…but she might know enough to pass the adventurer exam," I replied.

Maylee glanced at Rila for a moment and then at me. She still seemed confused about what was going on, so I explained to her the merits that came with becoming an adventurer.

"Am I going to become an adventurer?" Maylee asked.

"You can go on adventures at your own pace. If you don't like that kind of work, you could become something else," I said.

As Maylee was now, if some amateur hoodlum tried assaulting her, she was strong enough to handle them. Since she had learned self-defense and was stronger, she didn't need to become an adventurer, but…

"I'll do it." Maylee was eager.

Since she was motivated, we headed to the Adventurers Guild.

"Oh, Mr. Roland! And Miss Prima Donna and little Maylee. What are you doing here on your day off?" Milia inquired from behind reception.

Maylee, who had been holding my hand, hid behind my back right away.

"I'd like to register her as an adventurer today."

"You're registering Maylee as an adventurer... Huh?! But she's so little!"

"Yes. I think she's more than capable."

"Well, she can certainly take the test. If she does pass, we can register her."

Milia seemed concerned, but she still went through with the formalities. Maylee wrote out her name, age, and skill on a form placed at the reception desk.

*So Maylee can write. She must have received some education in the past.*

"We have a mana measurement and practical exam... Today's examiner is... Mr. Maurey, we have an adventurer exam."

The responsibility of examiner duties would rotate among staff members with adventurer experience every day. Today was Maurey's day.

"What? An exam? Sure, but I'm not gonna go easy on a runt." Maurey snorted as he looked at Maylee.

Seeing that, Maylee huffed and scowled.

"Tough luck you've got, kid, going against a former C-rank examiner like me." Maurey flicked her forehead amusedly.

"There's no need to go easy on her."

"I know, I know. You want me to give the runt a taste of reality 'cause she's stuck in daydreams, right? You want me to get her to give up on bein' an adventurer, I take it? I guess you could say that's just all in the day's work of a guild employee. Ahhh, it's a tough life."

Maurey sure seemed to be enjoying all of this. Apparently, he was the type who liked to pick on those who were weaker than he was. As Maurey repeated that sentiment again and again, Rila glanced at him and then, with a choice expression, said, "Adventuring is so much more difficult than any little one would think… It's kinder to show the powerless what's what."

Grabbing his coat and a wooden sword, Maurey quickly headed outside. The man only ever looked cool when he was leaving. He seemed to be trying to show off for Rila.

"Knave, I am prepared for a good laugh."

"Please don't."


We followed the former C-rank adventurer all the way to a field outside town.

The mana management was to come after this practical part of the test.

"In this adventurer exam, you can use a weapon, magic, or anything you want. Just do whatever you'd like, okay?"

Maurey leaned his wooden sword against his shoulder, tapping it a few times.

I handed a dagger to Maylee.

"Use this. I bought it for the exam."

"Roland…thank you."

I'd picked out one that seemed like it would be easier for Maylee to handle. It wasn't even six inches long. As it was an actual bladed weapon, I told her to keep it in the sheath.

With a resolute exhale, Maylee pumped herself up and gripped the hilt with her little hands.

"…I do wonder whether things will turn out all right…," Rila muttered.

I also felt a slight sense of parental affection for the child.

*Fwsh.* Maylee charged forward. She was short and quick, highly desirable traits for assassins.

"I'm sure she'll be fine," I said.

"Oh, uh, I don't mean her—"

When Rila attempted to continue, Maurey brought down his wooden sword.

"Hngh!"

*Fwsh.* Maylee changed her trajectory and dodged the attack.

*…Those movements…*

Maylee had taken Maurey from behind with no small amount of deftness. Maurey realized that Maylee had instantly exited his field of vision and reappeared behind him, but by then, it was too late.

"Back Slash!"

*Slap!* Maylee directly attacked Maurey's butt with the dagger.

"Gahhhhhhhhhhhhhhhh?! My ass, my ass—"

"Back Slash!" Maylee moved into his blind spot again and attacked.

"YeeEEEEEEOUCH!"

"Back Slash!"

"Gahhhhh?! Why're you only aiming for my ass?!"

I had told her that opponents hated to be attacked in a place where they'd already been injured—that had been the lesson for today.

"BAAAAAACK SLAAAAAASH!"

"S-stop already— I'm begging you—"

Maurey tossed aside his wooden sword and surrendered.

After that, we returned to the Adventurers Guild for the mana measurement. Maylee's mana just barely didn't reach the standard level, but she was allowed to pass because it was understood that she had room for growth.

That evening, we had a humble celebration of her successful exam.

"Um, so! It happened exactly like you said, Roland! It was amazing! I hit him like this and like that!"

Rila and I listened to Maylee excitedly talk over dinner.

I knew this feeling.

It was *warmth*.

◆

It was the day after Maylee had become an adventurer. Rila accompanied Maylee to the Adventurers Guild in the afternoon.

"Roland! A quest!" Maylee called out to me in a loud voice. I wasn't even at the reception desk.

"Maylee's so cute…"

"Watching her is so soothing…"

"Seeing a little adventurer is so heartwarming…"

The staff and other adventurers gazed tenderly at Maylee.

Since I had been called by name, a coworker vacated a spot at reception for me. She gave me a nod, and I took the seat.

"So your first quest, then."

"Uh-huh. I wanna do lots and loooots of Back Slashes."

When he heard the name of that technique, Maurey jolted,

ducked his head, and slunk away. Apparently, it had been traumatic for him.

"There are no battle quests for an F-rank adventurer like you, Maylee. I explained that yesterday, didn't I?"

As I took her adventurer permit and tried looking for an F-rank quest, I heard the loud sound of several heavy sets of hooves outside. Five knights clad in armor came into the guild.

"Found you."

They were looking directly at Maylee.

Their armor clattered as they approached. Every single one of the knights sported full-face helmets and the coats of arms of a noble.

The adventurers present in the guild all gulped.

"Hey, those aren't the lord's, are they...?"

"Yeah, it's Lord Bardel's Order of Chivalry..."

Count Bardel Algot. He was the feudal lord who managed several towns and villages, including Lahti.

Maylee ran behind Rila.

"Do you have some business here?" I asked.

A knight who seemed to speak for the others shook his head. "I apologize for the commotion. We were looking for this child."

Since they had sent an assassin after her, I'd thought that whoever was searching for Maylee already knew where she was. While it was knights coming for her this time, I still hadn't expected the feudal lord to be the one seeking her.

"Lord Bardel is waiting for you. We're going home."

Maylee shook her head. "N-no...! I...I'm staying here!"

Rila abruptly spread her arms to keep the knights away.

"Is it the job of knights to frighten young children? Have you no shame?"

This was a demon lord. Even if she had no mana and couldn't use magic, her presence alone was extremely intimidating. Those surrounding her were taken in by her intensity. Even the knights flinched slightly.

"Our lord has told us to use any means necessary to bring her home. Get out of the way!" The lead knight drew his sword at his hip. His comrades followed suit.

Things quickly devolved into panic in the guild. For a knight to unsheathe his sword spoke to the weight of Lord Bardel's order.

"You're turning your sword on an unarmed woman and child..."

I leaped over the counter and stood in front of Maylee and Rila.

"Stand down! This isn't a matter that some guild employee should be involved in—"

"I thought knights were a little more dignified than that."

My words seemed to agitate the knights. They gripped their swords tighter.

Depending on the region, a lord was basically the law incarnate. If one proclaimed that crows were white, then the crows in that territory would be white. It seemed Bardel was willing to use that power to bring Maylee back to him.

The knights brought down their readied swords with vigor. In the blink of an eye, we had started an exchange with life on the line. To me, that much was no different from an invigorating morning walk. I brought my fist to bear on the lead knight's face, shattering his helm. The knight flew away, and his back hit the wall, making a terrific racket.

"—Guh…"

He fell to his knees. I'd likely broken his nose and a few of his teeth.

The other knights, taken by surprise, had frozen on the spot. One of them came back to his senses and quickly ran away. Once they realized they were no match, the rest would flee, too. It was a remarkably good decision. I was sure that first guy would live a long life.

"Hey, hey…! That employee just sent one of the lord's knights flying!"

"Doing that to the knights under the lord's direct control is no different than threatening the lord himself!"

"What's he thinking? This whole thing could've ended if he'd just handed over the kid. How could you defy the lord's knights—?"

Adventurers, now spectators, began to offer some comments. When I looked at them, they quickly shut up, however.

"Ha-ha-ha, ah-ha-ha-ha-ha. How delightful!" Rila laughed.

"Hey, you!"

The knight collapsed on the floor raised his head. Just as I expected, his nose and mouth were bloody.

"Hmm. What a handsome man you've become. Though I have no idea what your face might have looked like before."

"Hey, Rila, stop with the sarcastic remarks."

Spit flew out of the knight's mouth as he shouted, "You dare obstruct the mission of Lord Bardel's emissary?! Moreover, you act in open resistance to us?! This is tantamount to rebellion! We shall have your head! Your head, I say!"

The guild stirred with unrest.

"Out of all things, you want to sentence this man to death…? Ha-ha-ha, guh-ha-ha…" Rila frantically tried to hold back her laughter.

"…You want my head? All right. I'd like to see you try to kill me."

With unmatched speed, I zipped over to the man and leaned down at him.

"If you can."

Startled at my sudden approach, the knight dropped his eyes as though unable to endure the pressure I exuded.

That was when it happened.

A somewhat pudgy man had made his way in.

"I was waiting in the carriage thinking you had finally found Alias. What a disgraceful sight to bear. Pitiful."

It seemed the escaped knight from earlier had called him in.

"It's the lord…"

"Count Bardel—"

*I see. So that's Lord Bardel.*

I recognized him.

"You made me toil so. We're going home, Alias."

Maylee was clinging to Rila tightly and wouldn't budge.

"Aristocrat, she says she will not go with you." Rila regarded Lord Bardel contemptuously.

"Hmm? Beautiful red hair, a lovely face, a gorgeous body… Hey, you, come with Alias, why don't you? I'll treasure you to my heart's content."

As he gave a shallow grin, Lord Bardel reached a hand toward Rila.

*Slap!* Rila smacked his hand down.

"Guh?! Y-you hit my hand—what irreverence!"

"Shush, you boor! You are the one showing irreverence… And the only one allowed to touch my bare skin is that man there!" Rila pointed at me.

"That man…? What? He's nothing but an ordinary guild employee."

As Lord Bardel snorted, I gave him a small nod.

"Lord Bardel…is your elder brother in good health?"

"What are you sputtering about? My brother drank poison six years ago and killed hims—"

After his older brother had taken his own life, Bardel had assumed his elder sibling's title. Milia had mentioned in the past that the town had become better after that exchange of power. So that older brother must not have been a very good lord. I didn't actually know much about the previous lord.

What I did know, however, was that an older sibling was merely an obstacle to one of ambition.

…There was no way the elder Bardel was in good health, because I'd killed him.

At this very man's request, I had made it seem like a suicide.

I took off my glasses, and Lord Bardel seemed to recognize me, for his face paled.

"Wha—? Wh-wh-what are you doing in a place like this—?!"

I plastered a gentle smile on my face.

That must have given Lord Bardel quite the fright. When I approached him, he fell flat onto his rear.

I drew close and whispered, "If you would be so kind as to overlook this child you call Alias, I will also overlook the terrible deeds you did to her. I will not speak of the aforementioned incident for the rest of my life. I will tell no one that you used underhanded methods to attain your position. After all, protecting secrets is part of the job."

Then again, I'd already quit that vocation.

Lord Bardel nodded vigorously several times. "O-o-o-o-o-o-of course! Naturally! I don't mind that at all! P-please do what you will with that child! And I am counting on your discretion in the other matter you mentioned as well…" The lord proceeded to prostrate himself.

""""Lord Bardel?!""""

An exclamation of distress erupted from the knights.

"Also, that knight over there told me I was sentenced to death," I added.

Just as he was raising his head, Lord Bardel hurriedly brought it low again. "I—I—I apologiiiiiiiiiiiiiiiiiiiiiiize! There is no way we would level such a punishment against you. I will give him a talking-to later. Please, please… I just beg for your mercy…!"

Guild employees and adventurers alike were in an uproar.

"Wh-what?! What is going on here?!"

"He punched a knight across the room and told one of them to *try* killing him…"

"He's got to be somebody important if a lord is bowing to him."

I was really drawing way too much attention. I grabbed Lord Bardel's arm and forced him up.

"Please stop, sir," I insisted.

I patted Bardel on the back and walked him out of the guild.

"I-if anything ever troubles you in the future, please tell me anytime…!"

"No thank you. That really isn't *normal*."

With those parting words, I watched the carriage and knights on horseback depart.

◆

After that, Lord Bardel told me everything about Maylee.

"That child is the princess of the Duchy of Bardenhawk… As you are aware, it was overthrown by the demon lord army, and the nation itself is gone; however, it seems that the region is somehow making an attempt at a revival."

There were nine countries in the world. The Duchy of Bardenhawk was one of two that had disappeared for one reason or another.

"The girl you call Maylee is Alias…Princess Alias Bardenhawk. When her nation was conquered, it seems that she somehow escaped, but according to the slave dealer, she seemed to be alone…"

Grim as it was, the slave dealer happening upon Maylee may have been what saved her life. Once she was passed into their hands, she at least had a way to survive, if barely. Then Maylee had been sold over to Lord Bardel.

"I realized that she was a princess because she carried a small brooch with the royal family's coat of arms engraved into it. It seemed she had already forgotten who she was by the time the slave dealer had come across her... Something rousing must have happened to her... More so than the girl's heritage, I believe the slaver brought her to my lands out of pity, as the war had not reached my territory..."

Such was how Maylee had ended up living her days as Lord Bardel's slave. It seemed Lord Bardel had planned to use Maylee to someday advance his political schemes. He had sent an assassin our way in order to secretly bring the girl back to him.

Bardel certainly seemed to possess no small amount of ambition.

Later that night, after Maylee had gone to bed, I recounted what I'd learned to Rila over some wine. I told her that Maylee was the princess of a ruined foreign country and had lost her memories due to the things the demon lord army had done. Rila, who sat next to me on the sofa, held my arm as she listened.

"What do you think?" I asked.

"Mm-hmm... There might be others who are searching for Maylee...," Rila pondered aloud.

"We could look into it, see if we can find them."

"How would you do that?"

"I could try asking King Randolf or—"

"...I suppose that is one way."

We both agreed that was the best plan.

Despite Rila and me having discovered Maylee's origins, we weren't enthused about the idea of giving her up. Rila put her head on my shoulder. We held hands and entwined our fingers without saying anything.

I wondered what this melancholy chill going through my chest was.

When I stroked Rila's hair, I could smell her scent. When we looked at each other, I saw my face reflected in her red eyes. When Rila cast her gaze down, I realized how long her eyelashes were. We kissed and gently moved apart. It seemed Rila was feeling that same curious gloom.

I tasted Rila's lips again. I put my arm around her as she draped her arms over my neck and straddled me. I felt Rila's breasts under her clothes. She twitched but still kept kissing me. In order to drown out the coldness in our hearts that silently fell like snow, we sought each other's warmth.

# ◆Maylee◆

How long had it been since that day? Maylee remembered it now.

She had recalled who she was and what had brought her here...

Had the memory returned before she'd gone to bed? Perhaps while she'd been in special training with Roland? Or maybe it'd come when she'd been playing with Rila? Maylee couldn't be certain. All she knew was that she remembered now.

She had a kind father, a beautiful mother, an older brother, an older sister, and a younger brother. Back when they lived in the castle, they wanted for nothing. Those were warm and happy days.

Supposedly, everyone in her family had died, but something in Maylee's mind told her there was a chance some of them may have survived. Unable to stand the thoughts of her past, Maylee had hidden them away from herself—frozen and forgotten. The warmth of a certain pair had thawed those memories out once more, however.

That night, Maylee went to Roland's room and snuck into his bed.

"What's wrong?"

Roland awoke from the slightest of sounds, but Maylee knew he would never tell her to leave.

"Nothing."

Creeping in like a kitten seeking warmth, Maylee squeezed herself right onto Roland's chest.

He stroked her hair. Wanting attention, Maylee pulled Roland into a hug.

"Ahem, R-Roland...? I—I went to take a bath... D-did I keep you waiting...?"

When Maylee heard that voice and peeked her head out from under the covers, she spied Rila wrapped in a single towel.

"Rila, you have to wear your pajamas or you'll catch a cold."

"Gah?! M-Maylee?! What are you doing in his bed?! We won't have a chance to spend the night together for a while, so I was in the mood for it today... Guh... I was planning for a full course until morning..."

Rila groaned as she let her towel flutter to the floor. After donning some underwear, she climbed into the bed.

Maylee ended up squished between the adults.

"Rila, I can see your boobies."

"Worry not. I do not mind, as long as it is in bed."

"Roland, are you going somewhere?"

"Yes, I'll be out for about two days."

"Where are you going?"

"…To work."

"You and I shall look after our abode together, Maylee."

"If you get bored, you can take on a quest at the guild," Roland said.

Maylee, suddenly finding herself rather sullen, hugged Roland tight again. From behind her, Rila hugged Roland, too, sandwiching Maylee in the middle. She could barely breathe, but it wasn't an unpleasant feeling.

"It's warm."

"Isn't it?"

"But I can't breathe."

When Maylee awoke the next morning, Roland had already gone off to work and was nowhere to be found.

◆

"Hey, King Randolf, wake up. Hey!"

I slapped the snoring king's cheek.

"Ngh? ……AhhhHHHHHHH?! R-Roland? What're you doing here?!"

I was in the king's private chambers. It was late at night. Having figured I'd be turned away if I applied for an audience during the day, I had chosen to come at this hour when I knew the king would be available.

"What a fright you gave me... Wh-what business do you have...?! You didn't get a request to kill me, did you...?!"

"I told you that I quit being an assassin, didn't I?"

"Ah, yes, I suppose you did," King Randolf said, putting on a nightgown that was close at hand. "My word, you're terrifying. The fright from catching sight of you in the dark is nothing to scoff at, you know. You might be worse than the grim reaper...," grumbled the king. "So what business do you have with me? Were you not the one who said it was unlikely we'd ever cross paths again?"

"I have a private request for you, rather than one as an assassin. There's something I want to make sure of. Asking you seemed like the best way to find out."

"What is it...?"

I filled the king in on the situation with Maylee.

"The princess of the Duchy of Bardenhawk, you say..."

"The Felind royal household had a connection with them, did it not? I want to know if there are any survivors. Any information would do. Is there anything that's come your way?"

"...I had Lady Leyte Bardenhawk under my protection for a time."

"You mean Maylee's mother? Where is she now?"

"Yes. With the backing of Felind Kingdom, she has headed back in order to restore the duchy. I do not know the fate of the others..."

"...I see. Then please tell Leyte Bardenhawk this: I am protecting her daughter."

I told the king where to find my home. With so few houses in its vicinity, it was unlikely to be difficult to spot.

"I will be indebted to you for this," I said.

"I already am deeply indebted to you, and this hardly settles my account."

"No, that was to me as the assassin. This time, I'm asking you for this personally."

"Ever the honest man, Roland. In that case…I have a matter that could settle what you owe."

"All right. What is it?"

"It concerns my daughter, the first princess and hero, Almelia."

After I finished my consultation with King Randolf, I made for home.

I told Rila everything, and we prepared ourselves for what was to come.

*Rattle, rattle, rattle.* Two days later, the sound of wagon wheels approached the house before coming to a stop. In the middle of breakfast, I exchanged a look with Rila and then stepped outside.

At our doorstep was an old carriage, four knights who looked like guards, and the four horses they had ridden in on. A lady borrowed the hand of the coachman as she alighted from her conveyance.

I bobbed my head slightly to her.

"My name is Roland Argan. I usually work at the Adventurers Guild as an employee."

"I am Leyte Bardenhawk."

She picked up her skirt and gave a motion of greeting.

Rila had brought Maylee out of the house, leading her by the hand.

"—Alias." Leyte's eyes watered as she caught sight of the little girl.

"Mother."

Rila and I looked at each other. It seemed Maylee's memories had returned at some point. I was glad she hadn't asked who this person with a carriage was.

Leyte ran over to her daughter and took her in an embrace.

"I'm so glad, so very glad. What a relief…"

"WaaaaaAAAAAAH." Maylee started to cry loudly.

Thinking back on it, Maylee had seemed unusually cooperative for her age, and she hadn't ever cried. Apparently, she had finally returned to her true self—Alias. She hadn't uttered so much as a single complaint during my training sessions.

"How—how can I possibly repay you…?" Leyte said between sobs.

"Don't worry about it. We only looked after her for a couple of weeks," I replied.

"That isn't the case at all. King Randolf informed me of what had happened. It pains me that I cannot properly thank you—"

"I didn't take her in expecting remuneration."

Leyte offered her gratitude a countless number of times.

"I shall never forget this for as long as I live."

After saying that, she pulled Maylee by the hand to try to get into the carriage, but Maylee wouldn't budge. Guessing what was going on, Leyte kindly told her, "Go say your good-byes," then got into the carriage.

Maylee turned around back to us. I thought she had finished crying, but her eyes were still full of tears.

"Roland…"

"Yes."

"Rila…"

"Mm-hmm."

Lips trembling, Maylee said, "Thanks, both of you…"

She rubbed her eyes again and tried to stop crying but couldn't.

"—I was happy—"

Rila bit her lip. "Yes. Us too."

Tears streamed down Maylee's cheeks, and as a whine escaped her throat, she said, "It was warm. And…I remembered something important… Also—also, now I can run a lot. I also became an adventurer—I had lots of fun with you two…"

Maylee ran to us with swollen, puffy eyes.

We got on our knees and hugged her close.

"WaaaaaaaaaaaAAAAHHH—"

I patted the inconsolable girl's hair. Rila nuzzled her cheeks against Maylee's, looking about ready to cry herself.

"This isn't good-bye forever, Maylee…Alias Bardenhawk. You can visit whenever you'd like," I said.

"Uh-huh." Maylee nodded several times. "I'll come back…and send letters…so make sure you answer…"

"Of course."

"Also, I'm going to make you my prince, Roland…so you have to treat me nicely like you do with Rila."

"Hmm. All right."

"What are you *all right*ing about?" Rila punched me in the side.

Maylee's tears finally dried, and she broke into a smile. She bid us good-bye as she got into the carriage and left. Both Maylee and Rila waved to each other for a long time. After losing sight of the carriage, Rila finally burst out sobbing. I pulled her in close.

The cloudless sky was bright blue. I remembered that *maylee* meant blue skies. I still felt that melancholic twinge in my chest, but this time it wasn't quite so unpleasant.

# 11
# How to Use a Skill

Days had passed since Maylee left.

I'd been working as usual while Rila did her own thing at home. Whenever she grew bored of that, she would tell me, and I would turn her into a cat so that she could come hang around my office.

"Mr. Roland...you've seemed down in the dumps lately," Milia observed as I was filing some papers.

"I'm down in the dumps?"

"Yes. Is it because Maylee left...?"

I wondered if that really was the case. I certainly didn't feel all that depressed. I'd told everyone at work that Maylee had gone back to live with her parents and that we were no longer taking care of her.

"I'm a little sad inside. It's a strange feeling," I admitted.

It was true that I'd stopped feeling that *warmth* ever since Maylee had left.

"Mr. Roland, that's what you call being lonely."

*I see. So this feeling is called loneliness.* I was certain that was what I'd been experiencing. As though I'd discovered a missing puzzle piece, I suddenly felt more assured. Rila and I had been lonely the last few days.

Iris had asked me for an explanation regarding the conflict between Maylee and the aristocrat Lord Bardel. In the privacy of her office, I told her the entire story. Everyone had been expecting the branch manager to scold me for acting violently in the office, but she actually did the exact opposite.

*"You seem more an ally of justice than an assassin."*

I doubted that any ally of justice would kill people for a living, but I accepted the compliment anyway.

"Um—! Just one more time, please! I'll work harder at magic and study more—"

"You may say that, but…"

A boy had his head lowered and was making a plea to a receptionist.

"I want to become an adventurer!"

"A failure on the exam is a failure. You're free to try the test another time."

I took interest in the exchange, and as I listened in, Milia informed me of the details. "He failed the adventurer exam earlier, but apparently, he refuses to give up. He came by yesterday, too."

Anyone could take the adventurer exam as long as they weren't a felon. In order to pass, you had to meet a certain base standard and have your abilities affirmed by a proctor. Those disqualified could retry only after half a year—as was written in the employee manual. This long waiting period was to encourage a failed entrant to train and grow stronger.

I gathered the results of the adventurer exam and thumbed

through them. There was only one person who had failed the exam after Maylee had taken it. It was a fourteen-year-old boy named Geppetto.

"…"

*Hmm. I see…*

Exam papers usually listed an applicant's name, age, weapon specialization, skill (if one had been identified), magic measurement value, and the proctor's name.

"The guild will be closing now, so you'll have to leave for today."

"…Yes, ma'am…" Geppetto's shoulders slumped as he left.

Closing time came, and, done with work, I left the office. I heard Milia call out from behind me, "Oh, huh—? Has anyone seen Mr. Roland?"

"Argan just headed home," one of our coworkers replied.

"Whaaat? He heads home too early… I wanted to have dinner with him today."

I found Geppetto sitting on the stone steps that led up to the guild's front door.

"You can't wait half a year?" I asked him.

He lifted his head when he noticed me.

"You're from the guild, right? …No, I need to hurry and become an adventurer so that I can give my mom a comfortable life…"

Becoming an adventurer did present the possibility of getting rich quick, but the likelihood of that happening was rather low. In that respect, adventuring wasn't very different from gambling.

"I was too weak… I failed the exam."

It was a male staff member who'd proctored the test. As far as I knew, there hadn't been anything off about it, either. Geppetto had been born and raised in Lahti. From what I gathered, he and his mother were only just barely getting by.

"I once saw the hero fighting the demon lord army from afar. I guess I wanted to be like her. She mowed right through large crowds of monsters and the demons with her sword—it was amazing," Geppetto said.

*Is that why he chose to use a sword?* Back during my time with the party of heroes, Almelia had also relied on her flair for swordsmanship, which left her fighting style very crude.

"I was curious, so I took a look at your exam results, Geppetto... It seems that your skill is Stick It Through."

"Yeah. I wanted so badly to be like the hero, but my skill is so worthless... If I'd only been given a better one..."

With few exceptions, everyone possessed a skill of some kind. Just as I had Unobtrusive, Geppetto had Stick It Through.

"Would you please show it to me? Your skill, that is?" I asked.

"Huh? I suppose I can..."

You had to be creative. No matter what kind of trash skill you had, what mattered was how you used it. Actually, unlike mine, Stick It Through wasn't such a bad skill to have. With a curious expression on his face, Geppetto followed me to a vacant lot in town.

"All right, here goes."

The young man unsheathed his sword and readied himself. His stance was full of openings, to the point that it was amusing.

"Hah!"

He thrust the sword forward with both hands. The skill he had invoked caused the tip of the blade to glow slightly. Then he slashed around a few more times, then stabbed, swiped, and showed me how he handled his blade.

"Just like it sounds, Stick It Through is a skill that specializes in piercing things. So you're using your skill when you thrust," I said.

"That's right," Geppetto answered jubilantly.

I looked around and found something perfect.

"Try using your skill on this."

"Uhhh. But that's not a weapon...?"

"Do you know how to use it?"

"I do. C'mon—I'm not dumb."

Not looking particularly excited, the boy took the shovel and stuck it into the ground.

*Kchunk—*

"Whoa! It went all the way in...!"

The shovel had buried nearly halfway down the handle.

"Th-this is amazing."

"That's the kind of skill you have."

"What? A-are you saying that my weapon is a shovel? Th-that's so lame... Super lame..."

Geppetto sank down to his knees, and his head drooped.

"Digging holes is incredibly useful. If you find yourself in a forest or cave with no safe place to rest, you can use the shovel to create your own spot. Pile up the earth and rock you dig out, and you'll have a wall."

"I—I guess that's true...!"

*Krnch, krnch, krnch, krnch.* Geppetto cut through the ground as easily as if it had been made of pudding.

The sight of it reminded me of something.

I was twelve years old when I'd first come up with an idea to make my useless loser skill into the strongest weapon in my arsenal. After hitting upon the idea, I'd been extremely eager to give it a try. I'd only started experimenting out of curiosity.

*If I move at full speed while activating my skill, how will my opponent react?*

Already possessed of physical prowess and advanced assassination techniques, I tested my new idea by using a pattern of attack that I had already found to be quite effective. It was what Maylee would one day call the Back Slash.

My opponent, a bear in the mountains, hadn't even stood a chance.

It was on that day that my honed abilities elevated my worthless skill, which merely made me seem forgettable, into a power that rendered me undetectable.

There was a by-product I hadn't been expecting, however. When I deactivated my skill following an attack, my real body seemed like an afterimage to my opponent. I would stop using my skill once I'd attacked, and the enemy would suspect that the real me was nothing more than an afterimage. Like some sort of magic trick, it seemed like a letdown when revealed, but it was impossible to follow with your eyes in real combat. Even if someone saw me for a split second, they would likely be dead in that same moment. An opponent who knew who I was and what kind of skill I used would still need to go to great lengths to deal with me.

That was why how you used a skill mattered.

"If the examiner has adventurer experience, then they're sure to accept the practicality of the affinity between your shovel and your skill."

"Ughhhh… But I can't take the exam for another half year."

"Why not take it at a neighboring town? There's no need to specifically do it here, is there?"

There was nothing that kept one from taking quests from somewhere other than where they'd been issued a permit, after all.

An applicant could take the test in any town.

"Huh? Can I really? Can I really go somewhere else to take it?"

"The next nearest guild is a bit far, but you can. The receptionist only told you that you couldn't take the exam for another half year in Lahti."

"I see… Thank you so much for teaching me so many things!"

Geppetto bowed his head, then ran off happily. I had wanted to show him how his skill could be used with some other tools besides a shovel, but he already had what he needed to pass the test. There were no other adventurers who were using shovels as their weapons. The rarity of such a feat would certainly earn him some attention.

A week later, Geppetto showed up at the office again.

"Sir!" the boy called out to me as I sat in the back.

In his hand, he held an adventurer permit.

"The examiner sung my praises! He said that the way I used my skill was very clever and was sure to lead me to success! I couldn't have done any of it without you. Thanks!"

"Well, that's fantastic."

"They said I'd be great at special quests…like digging up

minerals in the ground, excavation, building roads—stuff like that. They said I should work my butt off."

I had been thinking of showing him how to use some proper weapons, but this was probably good enough. This way, he wouldn't be involved in any really dangerous quests, something that his mother would likely be very thankful for.

"I'm excited to see where you go from here," I said.

"Ah-ha… Stop, you're embarrassing me," Geppetto replied.

I didn't mention it before because I didn't think it necessary, but are you interested in learning how to use a spear?" I asked.

Geppetto thought on it, then shook his head. "I'm going to adventure in my own way. I'll learn that if the need arises, though."

The boy grinned, and I returned the expression. The Stick It Through skill doubtlessly meant he'd never be a hero, but I didn't think it was bad to have adventurers like Geppetto around.

# 12
# The Unexpected Visitor

I was going about my work like any other day when the scene outside the office had grown rather imposing.

Several armored knights were loudly strutting around. I thought it was the feudal lord's Order of Chivalry again, but the crest was different. This group flew the colors of the Felind Kingdom's crest.

*If knights bearing that symbol are milling about…*

Suddenly struck by an ominous feeling, I left my seat right as the guild's front door swung open with a *BAM*!

"This is it, isn't it—?"

Those unyielding blue eyes and that long blond hair. She was wearing the exact same heroic outfit she had back when I was still traveling with her.

I righted my glasses, taking great care not to make eye contact.

"Ohhh?! I-it's the hero…!"

"Your Majesty, Princess Almelia—"

"What?! It's actually her?!"

*Tmp, tmp, tmp.* Almelia hurriedly approached reception. Milia was quivering, fear plain in her eyes.

"I apologize for the commotion. I heard that a man named Roland was here, so—"

I was only a few seconds from escaping the office when—

"There you AAAAAAAAAARE!"

I quietly glanced behind in the direction of the loud accusation. Almelia was pointing at me.

"No, you're mistaken."

"Then why are you trying to run?! And you're wearing glasses… Is that supposed to be a disguise?"

I heaved a resigned sigh and asked, "What do you want?"

"Hmph." Almelia snorted.

It was as though she was trying to say, *That much should be obvious.*

"I came here to become an adventurer."

I could feel a headache coming on and began to rub my forehead.

"Please refrain from doing that," I insisted.

"What? Why? Anyone can become one, right?!"

*Smack, smack!* Almelia hit the counter, causing cracks to form in it.

"Yeeeek!" Milia was cowering and looked as though she was about to cry.

*What is Almelia doing here…? Did the plan fail?*

Earlier, King Randolf's help resolving things with Maylee had indebted me to him.

The king had asked me for help on a matter of his own.

"It concerns my daughter, the first princess and hero, Almelia."

"…What happened?"

"I am thankful she returned home safe after the demon lord was slayed, but she has been entirely out of sorts ever since. When I asked a lady-in-waiting she's close with about it, the woman seemed to think it was because a certain person had disappeared from her life. Supposedly, Almelia and this other person had promised to live a happy life together once the war was over…"

"I see. Even after war, things can be quite chaotic. Losing contact is a pretty common occurrence. Do you want me to find this person?"

"No! It's you! You're the person! We're talking about you!"

To summarize, Almelia had been feeling down without me around. King Randolf told me that since I was the person in question, he wanted me to do something about it. I had no recollection whatsoever of making that strange promise, but I owed the king a favor, and I intended to repay it.

Almelia had held on to the hope that I was still alive. It just so happened that she was right.

Honoring her promise would be the nail in the coffin of my *normal life*, however. Remaining in the company of a hero princess was about as far from *normal* as you could get. I happened to like my current life anyway. After my talk with King Randolf, I consulted Rila on the matter.

"I see. What an afflicted man you are."

"I don't remember discussing with her what we'd do after the war, but Almelia thinks that I made some kind of promise. She doesn't know what happened to me after our fight, so she's been depressed."

"It's hardly a surprise that another woman would pursue a fine man such as yourself. How about this, then? You do not want to get involved with that hero, but she desires a reunion with you. The king also wants to see his daughter happy again. That being the case, why not give her closure? Make yourself out to be truly dead."

Rila's plan would put an end to Almelia wanting to get involved with me. While she'd no doubt be upset for a while, she would recover in time.

"Time will heal the hurt that comes with those who died in action," Rila added.

"Hmm. That might work," I said.

"Ha-ha. Of course it will."

"How might I convince her that I'm dead, though?"

"Within court-order-rank hepta, there is a type of illusion magic called Real Nightmare."

"I see. I'll use that spell to trick her."

"There you have it."

I'd never heard of such a spell before, but Rila explained it to me, and I grasped its mechanics easily enough.

"Hmmmm... That you learn it so easily reflects poorly on demons... What a portentous man you are..."

"*Real Nightmare*... I'm your owner, and you're my dog."

"...Wuff? Wuff-wuff! Nnnn, woof?"

Rila leaped at me on all fours, trying to play. I dodged.

*Hmm. So it's a form of hypnotism.* Rila no longer possessed any magical abilities, so the results on her were instant. The ensorcelled person would return to normal only upon being released by the caster or by being subjected to purification magic of court-order-rank hepta or above.

"Wuff-wuff?"

*Lick, lick, lick, lick, lick, lick. Smooch, smooch, smooch.*

"All right, I think that's enough."

I clapped my hands in front of Rila's face and brought her back to her senses.

"Hmm? Uhhhhh! You dare dishonor me?! Th-that was humiliating…!"

Now that I had a good sense of how to use the spell, I decided to go to the royal castle that same day.


Upon arrival, I slipped past the guards and snuck into Almelia's room. She was fast asleep in her bed. It was nice seeing her face again after so long. A tear trickled down from the corner of one of her eyes.

"Roland…"

"…"

I was no longer Roland the assassin. I was Mr. Argan the guild worker.

I steadied my wavering feelings and woke Almelia.

"…Huh—? Wh-who's there? …Roland…?"

"*Real Nightmare…* Roland died. He and the demon lord killed each other. There was no body because he escaped while wounded but later lost his strength and perished. I repeat, Roland is dead."

The magic took hold. It felt the same as when I'd done it on Rila. After a moment, Almelia's empty blue eyes returned to normal.

"Why…?" Almelia's throat burbled, and she started to sob. "No… Roland…be with me… I told you I wanted you to stay with me…and you promised… No…I don't want you to be gone…"

"I came to deliver the message. More than mourning him, you should be working to improve the country."

Almelia sniffled, and her tears refused to stop. "…I loved him… You can't just tell me something like that out of the blue… Roland…"

*The promise…*

Actually, I did remember something. Back when we traveled together, I usually treated Almelia like a child. Half driven by anger, she'd said to me:

*"After this battle is over, k-kiss…me. Not like a little kid, not something just superficial… Actually kiss me…"*

I had agreed to the young woman's request. It was like she'd been trying to overextend herself just to ask that, and I had found her effort endearing.

As I looked at her now, I realized she'd grown taller. Her hair was longer, too. She'd really become quite beautiful—though her chest was still lacking.

"I suppose I ought to keep at least one of my promises."

I grabbed Almelia's hands as she rubbed her eyes like a child. I wiped away her tears with the inside of my thumb. I put my arm around her back and brought her closer to me.

"…Hmm?"

I gently stole her lips. As far as I knew, this was a first for

Almelia. Not entirely understanding what was happening, Almelia eventually seemed to grasp the situation and responded to the kiss.

"A proper kiss… Have a good life, Almelia. I'm sure you'll accomplish great things."

With those words, I made my departure. Almelia looked half-conscious, as though delirious with a fever.

I leaped outside through an open window.

# ◆King Randolf◆

The royal castle, shortly after the death of the demon lord.

I was receiving a report from my favorite daughter, Almelia the hero, in my audience chambers. Elvie Elk Haydence, a paladin and daughter of the marquis of a neighboring nation, often acted as the group's spokesperson.

I had requested Roland travel with the party and, as expected, he'd done a splendid job of guiding them. His rumored strength had proven true, for he'd even defeated the demon lord. Almelia and the others seemed unlikely to enjoy taking credit for Roland's work, but they had to. Anything else would be problematic.

"The examiner verified it to be the demon lord's body," Elvie stated.

"You say it was *verified* to be the demon lord? Did you not all bring her down together?" I asked.

"We did not, Your Majesty… By the time we made it to the demon lord, she was already dead."

"It does not matter. Faced with you all, the fiendish demon lord likely gave up."

As I turned my gaze to each of the four party members, none of them looked satisfied. That much was to be expected.

Their eyes were practically saying, *Nu-uh, Roland was the one who did it...*

That man desired only a *normal life*. He hadn't wanted to be extolled as a great hero. I would not pull him out to the center stage by force. I had promised to fulfill any of his wishes as a reward for the request I had made. I had the obligation to make those wishes come true. Roland had completed his duty and had vanished.

...I wasn't sure how to describe him other than to say that he was a true professional. Man, he was cool.

"This discussion is over. As those who stormed the demon lord's castle, you have achieved a great feat. Leave the rest to the commanders of the allied forces and take a well-deserved rest."

"Father, Roland is... He disappeared before the final battle..."

*I see... So that's why Almelia looks so glum.*

The young mage Lina nodded eagerly. "...Your Royal Highn-y... Roland took a really long time going to the bathroom..."

*Did she just say* royal heinie?

Serafin, the high cleric, patted Lina on the head. "I'm sure Roland just really had to go."

*No, I'm pretty sure he didn't, Serafin.*

It wasn't only Almelia. It seemed everyone was worried about Roland's well-being.

"Your Majesty, in our humble opinion, we believe it was Roland who defeated the demon lord," Elvie asserted.

Such an assumption was only natural.

The man was insanely strong, after all…

That he could slay the demon lord single-handedly—there was something wrong with him.

Supposedly, this current demon lord was the strongest to have ever lived, too…

That it hadn't even taken Roland half an hour put him on a what-the-heck-did-he-even-do level of strength.

"There is no proof that Roland was the one who defeated her. Had you all not done what you did, no one would've been able to invade the demon lord's castle in the first place."

That's what Roland himself had told me.

"Father, that's incorrect."

"What is incorrect about it, Almelia?"

Roland had claimed that the entire party had worked together during the incursion into the demon lord's castle. It'd been give and take…

"I was…reckless and didn't pay any attention to the details while we were battling our way forward. Roland was always getting upset with me for being distracted. Even in the demon lord's castle, he saved me several times right before I stepped into a trap."

*Hmm…*

"How to use powerful moves, maintaining a psychological advantage over the opponent, the efficacy of subtle feints, drawing out the battle… Roland taught us all those things."

"It was the same for me, Your Majesty," Elvie the paladin added, raising her hand slightly.

As I remembered, she was the tank who served as the party's vanguard.

"As a coward with a penchant for running away, I learned from Roland how best to protect my allies. He was stern about how he phrased things, and there really were times when I wondered just who he thought he was, but…he was justified and, when it came to battle, his decisions always proved to be the correct ones. It's embarrassing to admit, but…all I did was listen to him and use my skill exactly as he told me."

*That Roland…* He'd been too humble when he'd made his report. I suppose he said what he did to make sure none of us would be left feeling uneasy. I always knew him to be terribly talented, but it seemed he was also attentive to the details of the follow-through.

He was downright praiseworthy.

"…Roland is like…a big brother… I like him… I wuv him so much… I want him to give me head pats again…"

*Me too, Lina. I* wuv *him, too.*

"It is just as you have heard, King Randolf. Had Roland not been there, we would've been little more than a mediocre party. Without him, we never would've been able to take the demon lord's castle. We may not have ever even reached it. No, we may very well have all wound up dead," admitted Serafin the high cleric.

He really was a great hero who stuck to behind-the-scenes work…

I wanted to thank him again, but I had no more a way of contacting him than my daughter did.

…In the days that followed, the party of brave maidens were

lionized as the heroines. The festival at the capital continued for an entire month and eventually, we welcomed a new normal.

Almelia, however, was not coping well. Desperate as she was, there were no leads on Roland's potential whereabouts. Much of her time was spent imagining whether or not he really had died and then trying to shake off such thoughts.

During that time, Roland actually spoke with me again, showing up during the night to ask for a favor. I didn't think that he had any obligation to repay me—he'd done so much already—but he insisted he was in my debt. That's why I'd requested that he somehow do something for Almelia.

It'd been a week now since I'd asked Roland to help my daughter.

Depressed though she'd been, Almelia had been coming to meals. Recently, however, she'd been refusing to leave her room.

"Why...? Sniffle... No... I can't believe he died... Ughhh...waaaah..."

She was sobbing like crazy.

*R-Roland...what did you do...?! Wait, maybe Roland has nothing to do with this.*

"High cleric Serafin, what do you make of Almelia's recent condition?"

I called the wasted high cleric into my private chambers. Apparently, she had been drinking around the clock since the end of the war. It'd gotten so bad that she was actually in danger of emptying my wine cellar. Her eyes were bleary, and her face was slightly red.

"Ngh... Yes, indeed... She might be in a state of magical dread, similar to the magic you'd call Fear."

"Wh-why, of course...! Since she is a princess and a hero, someone must be after my fair Almelia!"

"Yes, there is a magic used by demons called Real Something-or-Other that can put people into a trancelike state. Uguh..."

"Please, no vomiting!"

That meant some demon that'd survived was targeting Almelia. Naturally, they were no match for her in a fair fight, so they'd altered her mind somehow.

It made sense, and it explained why my daughter had been so depressed.

Serafin scrunched up her face, clearly battling the urge to hurl.

"Well then, could you purify Almelia and remove the spell that's been placed on her?"

"Y-yes... U-understoo...gweeeh—"

"S-somebody come quick!"


Later, Serafin used purification magic to free Almelia from the magical effect that had been placed on her.


"Roland's the one who snuck in here and did that to me...? What's with him?!"

I wasn't exactly sure what was happening, but I heard Almelia shout that from clear across the castle.

"Could this mean he sees me as...?! No waaaaaaaay! Whatever will I doooooo?! How dariiiiing!"

Her lady-in-waiting told me that Almelia had buried her face in a pillow and had been flailing her legs happily on her bed for a while now.

Whatever was happening, I didn't need the details.

All that was important was that Roland had done something, and Almelia's mood had finally picked up.

That was Roland for you. Professionals were never to be underestimated.

◆

I was sure that the Real Nightmare illusion spell Rila had suggested had worked. I had definitely told Almelia that Roland was dead, and she'd unmistakably believed it. Unable to understand where I'd gone wrong, I wondered if perhaps someone had purged the magic.

"What's with that scowl? There's a formal process for adventurer registration, isn't there? Or something like that? Hurry up and get started on it—c'mon," Almelia demanded.

This wasn't the kind of person I could leave to Milia, so I ended up taking the request.

"No wa— Regretfully, we cannot allow your admission."

"Why?"

"Not only are you a hero, you're also a princess. I do not think you should be going on adventures."

"I-it's fine. That's not a big deal."

Almelia averted her gaze.

Other staff members were whispering behind me.

"What's the deal? Is Roland friends with the hero...?"

"I'm not sure if they're friends, but it's pretty clear they've met before."

"He knows Almelia the hero princess…?"

"What exactly is Mr. Argan?"

"Maybe the hero saved his life during the war…?"

I decided to just let them gossip as they pleased; it wasn't as though any of them actually knew the truth.

That didn't lessen the heavy stares I could feel from every direction, however.

"I—I was so surprised…when you did that to me…but your feelings…uh…were very much received…"

Blushing, Almelia poked the tips of her pointer fingers together a few times.

"I'm not sure I recall the matter of which you speak," I replied.

"Could you drop that weirdly formal tone? Just talk to me like you used to."

Sighing, I acquiesced. "All right. Have you told King Randolf about this, Almelia?"

"My father has nothing to do with this."

"I see some things never change."

"Such as you treating me like a child."

*Chatter, chatter, chatter, chatter, chatter, chatter!*

My coworkers had formed a circle behind me and were speculating wildly.

"Hey, you hear that?"

"He's on a first-name basis with Lady Almelia."

"They know each other super well!"

"And look what's happening… She's fidgeting…and blushing…"

"They gotta be intimately involved. No doubt about it."

"You hear how casually he spoke about the king?"

"Maybe they're engaged?"

""""Ohhh, so that's how it isss…""""

*No. Entirely wrong.*

"That's odd. I heard that anyone can become an adventurer, though," Almelia said.

"Anyone can, but you have more important things to be doing," I shot back.

"D-don't think you can push me around just because you're wearing glasses! Actually, why are you even wearing glasses in the first place? I mean, they look good on you…"

*Then what's the problem with wearing them?*

"Roland, if you're an employee here, then you should listen to your superiors," Almelia insisted.

"Don't order me around."

"Hey, you can't talk to the princess like that."

"Y-you won't be the only one in trouble, Roland. As branch manager, my head will roll for this as well…!"

Turning back to look toward the branch manager's office, I found Iris quietly watching.

"Oh! Are you Roland's superior? I'm going to become an adventurer. Are you fine with that?"

"I can't exactly refuse, but—"

"What's your name?"

"I am Iris Negan. I oversee the Lahti Adventurers Guild."

"Really? Then I will make sure to remember that."

"You honor me."

With a smug exhale, Almelia haughtily raised her chin.

She was really giving everyone a good helping of her more ill-behaved side.

*Bam!* I thumped on the counter with a fist.

Almelia jolted and ducked her head.

"Adjust that arrogant attitude of yours. Iris is my boss. Don't be rude to her."

"Uh… I-I'm sorry…"

"Have you introduced yourself to Iris?"

"N-not yet…"

"You can't assume everyone knows who you are. Don't get too conceited."

"I-I'm sorry…"

Almelia immediately shrank down. She apologized for her presumptive actions and formally introduced herself. "I am Almelia Felind, first princess of the Felind Kingdom. There are many who call me a hero."

"I am well aware," replied Iris.

This time, it was the adventurers who began to excitedly whisper among themselves.

"She got an apology from the hero."

"I can't believe how the princess is acting around that guy."

"And he gave her a lecture like it was nothing."

""""Who is he…?"""""

There wasn't a single pair of eyes in the office that wasn't trained on Almelia and me.

"There you have it—your boss has consented to me becoming an adventurer," Almelia declared.

"Very well. In order to become an adventurer, you'll have to undergo a magical measurement and a practical exam. A proctor will judge your aptitude... Today, that responsibility falls to me," I said.

"What's that mean?"

"I'm the one who decides whether you pass or fail."

"Geh..." Immediately, Almelia grew anxious.

"The standard for aptitude varies based on proctor. So how about this: If you can win against me, then I will accept that you have the aptitude to be an adventurer."

The guild office broke into an uproar.

"I-if he wins...? But he's going against the hero...!"

"He just picked a fight with the strongest person there is!"

"What is this guy thinking?!"

"That's obviously impossible! What's even the point?"

Almelia was shaking her head rapidly from side to side. "That's totally unfair! No fair! Passing based on taking you on as an opponent...is impossible!"

"Is the hero giving up already?!"

"What is going on here?!"

"Isn't she the one who brought down the demon lord?"

""""Is this guy...really that strong...?!"""""

Almelia could've easily become an adventurer at some other guild, but she seemed quite fixated on the one where I worked.

"All I want is for you to acknowledge me, Roland," Almelia said.

"Then why bother becoming an adventurer?"

"...I just needed an excuse to see you... Get that through your head...you dummy!"

Almelia grabbed a pen and hurled it at me.

*Fwoosh.*

I plucked it from the air.

"I—I didn't see what happened…"

"What just happened?"

I returned the pen to its spot on the desk.

"Please don't throw the office supplies."

"Hmph…"

"We should start your exam. Let's go outside."

Urging Almelia on, I headed out of town.

We certainly had no shortage of spectators. There were the knights Almelia had brought along, some regular citizens, and the adventurers. There was such a crowd, it almost felt as though the whole town was watching.

Standing opposite me, Almelia sharply inhaled and slowly exhaled. It was a concentration technique I had taught her.

She drew her named sword, a weapon called Aizworz.

"Roland…I'm going to give this my all! I want you to acknowledge what I can do. And I'm going to become an adventurer!"

"Your feelings will not make this happen. I'm sure I taught you that. Feelings, aspirations, and desires require power to carry out… I will check to see whether you have what it takes."

I stuck my empty hands in my pockets and faced down Almelia's mighty sword unarmed and head-on. Beads of sweat formed on Almelia's forehead, and she held a tense breath.

"…Ugh."

When I stepped forward as though I was going for a stroll, she took a large step away from me.

Immediately, onlookers began to murmur among themselves.

"What's going on?"

"As soon as he got a little closer to her, she immediately jumped back."

"The hero…isn't able to attack."

Almelia wasn't a monster that blindly attacked out of instinct. She was doubtlessly examining the situation. As though she was starting over, Almelia calmed her shallow breathing and readied her sword again. There was no lack of determination in her—that much was certain. It was difficult to say that she was properly skilled enough, however.

I was glad I hadn't had her fight Rila while she was exhausted. If she had, she probably would've died. Almelia was giving off a fortified pressure. Spirit, valor, tenacity, bloodlust—all could be felt coming from her.

I returned her threatening aura in kind.

As Almelia shuddered, her face paled. The tip of her sword started to shake. Her breathing became ragged. Her abnormal amount of sweat spoke to the fact that she had learned how to tell who was more powerful even without having to cross blades.

I wanted to praise her growth.

As her knees started to give out, Almelia dropped her sword and put her hand to the ground.

"Huff…haaah, huff… No way… I thought I'd gotten a little stronger…haaah, haaah… I practically died twenty times…"

She had lost a few more lives than that, but who was counting?

"You were able to withstand my menacing aura for a whole

five seconds. I think you've become stronger compared to that one time when you fainted and wet yourself after being hit with it in battle."

"D-don't talk about that! I never wet myself! That was sweat!"

"You sure sweat a lot around your thighs."

"Shut up!"

"Anyway, I won. Unfortunately, I can't acknowledge you as an adventurer."

"Fine, I'm done! You're a dummy, Roland! You're too mean! Take a hint! I'll be back!"

After sticking her tongue out at me, she stomped back to town.

"Do as you please."

She shot me a bashful glance before running off.


"Mr. Roland, what kind of relationship do you have with Her Majesty the princess…? Sh-she's not your ex or something, is she…?" Milia asked after I'd returned to the office.

"We traveled together and defeated the demon lord."

"Ah-ha-ha-ha. Yeah right."

"I'm kidding. I was something like…a private tutor."

"Oh, I see… So that's how it is, then! That sounds about right! That's why you've got glasses," Milia reasoned, not quite hitting the mark.

Since I had been teaching Almelia the fundamentals of battle, it wasn't completely wrong, though.

For some time after Almelia's visit, I acquired yet another strange title: former royal tutor.

# 13
## Small-Fry Adventurers × 3 = ?

I looked at the adventurer permit, then at the woman sitting across from me.

Everly Torqus. Nineteen years old. An E-rank adventurer. Her weapon was a sword. Her protective gear consisted of a buckler on her elbow. Her skill was… Hmm.

She was the type of adventurer who was all over Lahti—what you'd call a low-class adventurer.

"You said you'd like to do a bigger quest?"

"Yes. I don't even mind if I end up with a useless party. I was wondering whether there's anything available."

When it came to party quests, her adventurer rank was really at the bare minimum. Forming a party created a collective level of ability that staff members judged. With a strong group, you could take on quests you normally couldn't otherwise. I wondered whether there was a party quest still needing a member. I flipped through the many collected files and looked for a quest that fit her desires.

*Waiting on one more. Please let this expire if someone good doesn't turn up, though.*

There was one quest slip that I found with a note tacked on to it. It was a D-rank quest that sought a party of bodyguards for a merchant and his goods. The minimum was three adventurers, and they currently had two, both of whom were F-rank.

While we were supposed to judge their strength as a group, even after adding another adventurer to their party, this was likely to end in failure. It depended on who the additional adventurer was, but I doubted anyone "good" would accept this.

If I forced Everly to take this on and the merchant died, suffered injury, or lost any of his stock, the responsibility for that would fall on the Adventurers Guild.

I felt bad for Everly, but rather than offer her a quest beyond her capability, it was probably safer to arrange a different quest that was better suited to her rank. Then again...

"What do you think of this one?"

"Rank D... Bodyguard a merchant and his merchandise... I-I'll do it!"

"Very well. Then I will go through the procedures."

Naturally, it was reckless to have three underprepared adventurers head out on the quest as is. The merchant wasn't leaving the town until tomorrow, however.

I knew the two F-rank adventurers. Based on how they fought, I was sure they had enough in them to tackle a D-rank quest.

Atolo, one of those two F rankers, happened to be in the Adventurers Guild already, so I called him over. He was a tall man in good physical condition. On his back, he carried a spear.

Right as I was discussing the quest acceptance with him, the last member of the party, a man named Uno, happened to walk in. In contrast to Atolo, Uno was petite and carried a longsword that didn't fit his stature.

"Everly here has joined the convoy quest you both applied for, so its conditions for acceptance have been fulfilled."

"N-nice to meet you."

Everly and the other adventurers exchanged handshakes.

I turned away from the counter.

Surmising that I was leaving my seat, Milia took over my post at the reception window. When our eyes met, she smiled as she formed an okay sign with her pointer finger and thumb. I bowed my head slightly at her.

"Um, sir, do you really think we can handle this...?" asked Uno, the one with the longsword.

Something like that was pretty hard to tell after just glancing at three random adventurers.

"Yeah, I was wondering that, too... Maybe I shouldn't have applied." Atolo seemed to feel the same way.

Everly also raised her hand. "S-same here... I accepted because it was recommended to me, but based on our lineup...I'm a little worried."

At this rate, the merchant who'd submitted the request was going to have to change his departure date or else hire guards using some other place as an intermediary. That'd mean our guild had failed him. They might not have believed it, but I was confident these three adventurers could handle the job.

As things were currently, it was impossible, however. The planned route was going to take them through a region that had recently become infested with thieves and bandits.

"Let's head outside. I'll coach you on some things," I said.

The three adventurers exchanged looks.

After making some preparations, I led the group to an empty lot on the outskirts of town.

"Just as each of you fears, you are a group of weak, low-grade adventurers with little experience," I stated.

"You…you sure have got a loud mouth."

"I already knew that."

"Y-you didn't have to put it so bluntly."

Uno, Atolo, and Everly each answered in turn.

"What's more, you bit off more than you could chew by applying for this quest. I imagine you all hoped to rely on some other, stronger member. You didn't even consider whether you'd slow anyone down or that you would cause trouble for others."

Admittedly, Everly had taken the quest only because I'd suggested it, but that was another matter.

"Ughhh…you're going too far!"

"Th-that's right. I applied thinkin' I could help out…"

"I'm sure we'll be fine as long as we work hard together."

Uno hollered, Atolo's mouth curled into a thin frown, and Everly looked slightly angry.

Rila had taught me a useful bit of magic recently. After casting it, four child-size assistants appeared. Apparently, this spell was called Shadow.

"Ahhh?!"

"What're these things?!"

"Did those little things appear out of nowhere?!"

My arms folded, I mentally commanded my four conjured servants to move.

"Scree!"

One of them gave Uno a good kick in the shin.

"Agh?!"

Another stole the spear Atolo had with him, while the third jumped and punched him in the face.

"Ack?!"

The last one lifted Everly's skirt.

"Eek?!"

Since she was unguarded, it also pulled down her underwear.

"S-stop!"

None of the shadows was particularly strong. In fact, they were quite weak. All it took was an attack of this level to reduce the three adventurers to a sorry state.

"You told me I'd said too much? That you meant to be helpful? That things would be fine as long as you worked hard? Please don't make me laugh. The real world isn't kind enough that you can get by on sentiment alone. First, please realize that you are weak. Then we can begin."

"D-don't just attack us out of nowhere."

"Do you think monsters would give you a heads-up?"

"…"

"Robbers and bandits wouldn't, either."

"B-but they wouldn't flip up my skirt or…"

"You died because you were distracted by your underwear—what an entertaining joke."

"Ughhh… But…I want to keep it cute…"

"If you're worried about that, please wear pants."

When it came to women, it wasn't as though things would end with a skirt being flipped or underwear being pulled askew if this had been real. She would likely be raped, gang-raped, abused until she was a rag, or sold into sex slavery.

I explained as much to Everly.

"""……"""

The group's earlier defiance quickly faded as they all lost their enthusiasm.

"'We are useless nobodies. We are worms who slow others down.' All right, repeat!" I ordered.

The trio stood at attention and parroted dutifully.

"""We are useless nobodies. We are worms who slow others down.""""

"Please don't forget those words. That will keep your attitude modest and will turn into a desire to improve yourselves."

With that handled, it was finally time to tackle the issue at hand.

"Now that you understand, I'm going to coach you. Follow my instructions closely."

"""Yes, sir.""""

I knew what their skills were and had prepared a few corresponding things for the group beforehand.

"Huh… Am I supposed to use this…?"

"I'd prefer my spear, though."

"So…you're having me wear pants after all, then…"

In order to check their skills, I had the three of them fight several times against a squad of five shadows.

The results based on their skills were exactly what I'd expected.

I could move my summoned helpers directly, but they could also move on their own if I gave them instructions.

"I'm going to head back to the guild. Please practice with the shadow squad on your own."

"""Yes, sir.""""

With how determined those three were, I trusted that they wouldn't abandon the exercise.


The next day, I introduced the merchant to the trio of adventurers.

"You're my guards... Thank you for taking the job, even if it's a quick one."

"""Thank you for hiring us!""""

The three adventurers had been picked on a lot by my shadow squad. In the end, however, they'd managed to best a group of six of them. Come the day of the quest, they all looked the part of seasoned soldiers.

They'd probably be fine now. I was still concerned about how they'd fare, though. That was why I'd snuck one shadow on the back of their wagon.

While it wasn't possible to maintain for long periods of time, I could share senses with the shadow.

As I worked, a different shadow sitting with its knees folded up at my feet twitched and tugged on my pants as it called in a low, screeching sound.

"Hmm? Ah, they've been waylaid."

I left my seat for a while and synced my senses with the shadow I'd had accompany the adventurers. I saw the wagon and six men who looked like bandits.

"Heh-heh-heh, looks like we've got ourselves a woman on board!"

"Guess we've got ourselves something to look forward to after killing the men—!"

The robbers smiled lewdly.

"Just as we practiced, you two."

"Got it."

"You can count on me!"

Uno and Atolo replied in turn to Everly's calm instruction.

The petite Uno started at a run. The longsword he once had had been replaced with a dagger.

"The hell is this pip-squeak?!"

Uno dashed right into the middle of the robbers who wielded sabers and axes.

"Take that!"

Just as I'd taught him, Uno used his skill to stop the bandits' attacks.

Uno's skill was Instant Acceleration. For less than a second's interval, he could increase his agility. Having deflected all incoming strikes, Uno countered with his dagger.

"Guh…"

"You better not underestimate us, you pip-squeak!"

A notable feature of Instant Acceleration was its short cooldown. Just about three seconds, in fact. All Uno had to do was survive for those few moments, and he could use his skill again.

"Damn! I can't get him!"

In an all-out brawl, there was no better skill to have.

According to Uno, he'd never fought in a party before. That's why he'd placed so much importance on his weapon's reach and offensive power. I understood his desire to fight safely, but that denied him the chance to take full advantage of his capabilities.

What I'd sought from Uno wasn't prowess at activating his skill but the courage to charge toward his foes.

The bandits were quickly falling prey to chaos as Uno cut through their ranks. While they tried to fight back, they were too concerned about hitting one another, putting them at a disadvantage.

"Now!"

"*Hahhhh!*"

At Everly's signal, Atolo readied his large, two-handed shield and charged in. That, too, was something I'd arranged. Previously, he'd been wielding a spear, but fighting with a shield suited Atolo's skill better.

His skill was Harden, which strengthened the toughness of objects. This made Atolo's way of battle rather simple.

"Hahhh!"

All he had to do was ram the shield into his opponents' faces.

*KRNK.* There came a dull sound followed by a scream.

Despite the shield being of cheap make, there wasn't a scratch on it. Having a giant man charge in with such a sturdy weapon packed quite a punch.

"Where're we supposed to attack him from—?!"

The large shield guarding Atolo's front meant that they could attack him only from the knees down. To compensate, he wore greaves. It seemed unlikely that the bandits would be able to deal with him in the middle of such a close-quarters fight. Blades bounced off the shield with resounding metallic echoes. Atolo thrust forward with the unlikely weapon, cracking the noses of those unfortunate enough to get hit.

Uno had gotten himself surrounded, and a slash bit into his back. "Gwagh?!"

Everly had been hiding behind Atolo. From her place of safety, she used her Heal skill. Uno's wound remained, but the bleeding stopped instantly.

Any robbers still able to move and get near Everly were repelled by her sword. The woman was fairly levelheaded so long as there were no strange distractions. Atolo couldn't see where he was going because of his shield, so Everly was directing him while taking in everything going on around her.

Truthfully, her swordsmanship was terrible. With the group of bandits in such disarray, however, she was afforded many chances to get in attacks.

"The enemies are—" Everly started, taking a look around. Not a single robber was left standing.

It had been a fine battle, exactly of the sort I liked—systematic, steady, simple, and uncompromising.

The three adventurers looked to one another and excitedly high-fived.

They made a good team.

The merchant, who had been watching from behind the wagon, emerged from his hiding spot.

"You're lifesavers… Thank you so much! You seem very well versed in fighting. I had my doubts when I heard how low you all were ranked, but it seems I had nothing to worry about."

"Actually, we were barely amateurs until yesterday."

"Our teacher taught us the basics of battle; that's how we got through this."

"I see." The merchant nodded. "Then you had a good teacher."

""""We sure did."""

Based on their tones, it sounded like I didn't need to worry about them anymore.

I cut off my link with the shadow.

No matter what skill you had, no matter what sort of adventurer you were, success depended on combination and coordination.

# 14

## Achievements and the Full-Time Staffer

"There's something I'd like you to do, Roland."

After we had closed the Adventurers Guild, we often held short meetings where Iris would give announcements. This time, she had specifically called me out.

"What is it? …If you're inviting me to dinner, I must politely decline."

"I-I'm not! Don't turn me down when I haven't even offered." Iris cleared her throat before continuing. "Up until today, we've been rotating which staff members handle the adventurer exams, right? From now on, you're going to be the only one who conducts them."

It seemed a strange decision. The office wasn't so busy that we couldn't afford the interruption that rotation caused.

Things were going just fine.

"Branch Manager, are you sure you can leave that up to Roland? The reason we swap people out in the first place is because we don't want things to get too lopsided based on one proctor's personal tastes," Maurey called.

"Yes, that's true," Iris replied. "But I've been collecting some data—have a look."

The documents she passed around contained a record of comparisons between the adventurers I'd tested versus ones who my coworkers had.

"Such a huge difference..."

"But there weren't any standouts among the adventurers who Mr. Argan passed."

"Actually, far from being talented...a ton of them failed the exam at other branches..."

"But despite that—"

On the sheet was a history of quest acceptance rates for the adventurers I had passed, as well as their average successes. It also detailed averages on how quickly my adventurers rose in the ranks.

"Mr. Roland, this is amazing! Most of the adventurers ended up rising to rank E within only a month!" Milia exclaimed, wide-eyed and loudly tapping her copy.

*That's enough, Milia. I have the same documents, so I can see that for myself.*

Iris hushed the excited staff.

"I think this makes things fairly plain. All the adventurers Roland passes are exceptional."

"O-one of the adventurers I remember Roland proctoring for... is already a C rank...," Milia said.

"Wait a sec, but Roland only started doing exams...two months ago."

"One of Roland's earliest approvals? They rose to rank C in only two months? H-how...?"

"That's super top-of-the-line!"

Memories of the first adventurer I had passed came to the forefront of my mind.

Milia pulled up the adventurer registry. In it was also recorded each adventurer's exam results.

"W-wait—it's this person. Please look! Right here!" she called.

Other staff members crowded around to peek at the records.

"Magic measure…E. That's no good."

"Hey, wait. The practical evaluation was also an E…"

"Isn't the passing cutoff for both a C…?"

"I would've failed him."

"Anyone would've."

I hadn't been stern in my evaluation of the applicant. The adventurer had shown me results from another failed exam, and the ability evaluation had been about the same.

""""This failed adventurer is the fastest person to ever rise to rank C?!"""""

Though there were standards, the person who had final say on whether someone passed was the proctor. I evaluated more than an applicant's abilities. I also observed their character. That particular adventurer had been a serious, honest, sincere, and hardworking boy.

When I'd told him he'd passed, he'd been just as surprised as anyone else. After the test, I'd gone over the strong and weak points I'd observed while administering the exam to him.

People who have a strong sense of their strengths and shortcomings are surprisingly rare. After I made sure he understood that, I gave him concrete explanations of how to compensate and how best to play to his strong suits. I also taught him what to look out for when embarking on solo slaying quests, as well as what role to take in a party and how to fight with one.

*"It's the first time anyone has explained so much to me so thoroughly...,"* the young man had told me, thoroughly moved. *"Just watch! I'll pay you back for passing me, sir! I'm going to work my butt off!"*

Evidently, he'd honored that promise.

It seemed likely that he'd previously been told by people at other branch offices that he wasn't cut out for adventuring.

Whether someone was suited for such a life depended more on their own motivation than anything else. Without that drive, even guild staffers couldn't force them to accept quests. No ambition meant no growth. No one could make you improve if you didn't want to. That's why I believed that bringing out an adventurer's motivation was part of the job.

"Have you done anything special during your exams?" Iris asked.

"Not especially," I replied. From there, I recounted how I usually conducted my tests.

The staff members were taken aback.

"You're going out of your way to do that...?"

"I don't think I could've given such precise tips, even if I'd wanted to."

"I knew you were different, Mr. Roland! I was sure of it—right from the start!" Milia said.

Iris nodded thoughtfully. "I'm convinced that the adventurers you pass make more of an effort after seeing how sincere you are."

"No, it's a result of their own hard work. I have nothing to do with that," I protested.

"Such modesty, even after all you've done...," one coworker praised.

"No, I'm not trying to be modest. I really believe what I said."

"It's not like you have nothing to do with the successes of the adventurers you pass... You never claim any of your own accomplishments," another staffer added.

"His sense of professionalism is kinda cool...," remarked a third.

Iris snickered at her subordinates' comments.

"Will you accept my proposal, then? I'd really like to entrust you with this responsibility."

"If you're okay with it, then I'll accept. Actually, I think that work will be more efficient if others don't have to spend as much time dealing with exams."

Applause broke out. A strange feeling overtook me; it almost felt a bit embarrassing.

# 15
# The Celebratory Feast

I was on my way home after it had been announced that I would be handling all exams.

"Mr. Roland…!" Milia called. She was chasing after me while cradling a paper bag.

"Let's celebrate! You've been appointed our full-time examiner, after all."

With a "ta-daa," she produced a bottle of wine from the bag. It was a fairly expensive kind, too.

"No, today I have to—"

"When something good happens, it's only normal to celebrate with everyone!"

"It's *normal*?! …All right, then. If that's the case…"

"Yay! ♪ …Wait. You're not doing whatever anyone tells you simply because they say it's normal, are you…?"

"You just said that it's a celebration with everyone, right?"

"Hmm? Oh, yeah. The branch manager will stop by a bit later, too. She's going back home to get changed first."

"Where are we doing this?"

"At your house."

*So it's normal to celebrate in the house of the person being celebrated.* I had slight reservations about this, but what other option was there?

"...All right. Let's go."

"Yay! ♪"

When we arrived at my place, we found Iris standing by the front door, fidgeting.

"Wow, you got here so fast!" Milia said.

"I guess I did. This is for the celebration." Iris handed me an expensive bottle of liquor.

Milia grinned. "You sure look fancy tonight, ma'am."

"Not in particular. This is normal for me."

She had redone her makeup and was wearing stylish clothes as well as a bracelet.

*I see... So this much is* normal.

"It sure seems to me like you're all psyched up, though," Milia commented.

"Watch your mouth," Iris shot back.

When we went inside, Rila scrambled noisily down the hallway.

"Welcome ho— Hmm? It appears we have visitors today. What a rarity."

"Nice to see you again, Miss Prima Donna."

Rila greeted Milia with a slight bow of the head. "...What? Are you planning a foursome or something?" she asked.

"No. Apparently, we're celebrating," I replied.

"Celebrating?"

"I'll explain. Nice to meet you. I am Roland's boss, Iris Negan."

"Ah yes. I recognize you."

Iris seemed dubious of that claim. Rila had undoubtedly grown familiar with Iris's appearance because she came and went from the office as a cat so regularly.

Iris filled her in on what had happened back at work.

"Oh-ho. So that is why you are having a banquet, then. Mm-hmm, not a bad idea."

For some reason, Rila seemed pleased.

"Miss Prima Donna, would you mind lending us your kitchen?"

"Hmph. You dare step into my castle? I admire your pluck, young maiden."

"…What are you talking about? We're just going to make food. All we're doing is cooking."

After a brief exchange, Rila and Milia disappeared into the kitchen. In their own sort of way, they seemed to be getting along well enough.

"Um, Miss Prima Donna, what is this thing in the pot?"

"It is a soup I put great pains into making. A single taste will have anyone kneeling."

"Um…I think it'd be more likely to send someone keeling… Hey! Make sure you're feeding Mr. Roland decent food!"

"Damsel, hold your tongue! Even I draw the line somewhere."

"Enough already! You're in the way, so just get out."

I heard the two yelling at each other from the kitchen. Eventually, Rila came into the living room, looking like she'd been banished from a demon lord's castle.

"That accursed maiden understands nothing… Oh, I seem to have neglected introducing myself. I am Rileyla Diakitep. My thanks for always looking after this man," Rila said to Iris.

"Not at all. He seems to have no end of helpful surprises."

While snacking on jerky, Rila and Iris drained their glasses of wine.

"...So what exactly is your relationship to Roland?" Iris inquired.

"That is obvious, is it not? I am something like his partner."

"His partner... Huh? What?"

I had only just finished explaining that Rila and I had met each other while traveling.

*Partners... We're partners?*

"There is no need to be so flustered, Iris. I am generous. It is natural for a female to seek good stock. I do not intend to investigate where he chooses to sow his seed... As long as he makes sure to come back to me...," Rila declared, though she spoke that last bit in a shy whisper.

Her face was red—probably because of the alcohol.

"Hmm, I see. So that's why he always turns me down when I invite him to dinner."

Rila snickered at Iris's remark.

"Miss Prima Donna, what are you gushing about? Now I'm kind of depressed!"

Having brought over some food, Milia joined in on the conversation.

"A girl who has scarcely finished wet nursing is not even on the same level. You might as well fall to your knees before me, virgin."

*It hasn't been that long since you lost your virginity, though...*

"Grrrrr...!"

*Plonk.* Milia sat right next to me and gulped down in one go the drink she'd poured herself.

"Ahhh… After seeing how unskilled you are at cooking, Miss Prima Donna, it's clear that I'm much better and definitely more preferable."

"I'm not that fussy when it comes to food," I commented.

So long as I got the right nutrients, it didn't matter much to me.

"There, you see?"

"Grrrrr…!"

We partook of the drink and Milia's food.

The conversation turned to work and past events. We had no shortage of things to talk about.

Each of the women had their own sort of elegance. One a flower high above one's reach, another a dandelion at one's feet, and the third a large, blooming rose.

Rila, who had been drinking happily, was the first to go down. In an attempt to keep up, Milia was the second to fall. I took each of them to a bed so they could sleep off the alcohol.

Iris and I continued to chat while we polished off what remained of the wine.

Our eyes suddenly met. Actually, it was more like I'd felt a gaze boring into me and I looked up, wondering what it was.

*Smooch.* As though trying to gauge the space between us, Iris leaned in and ever so slightly grazed her lips against mine.

"…You didn't try to get away. What a naughty man you are."

"You know what I used to do. I think you're aware of just how naughty I am."

"Hey… Is seducing women one of your specialties, too?"

"It was an option for obtaining information… I suppose it depends on the situation… If there was a need for it, I'd do it."

Iris pushed on my shoulders to knock me down on the sofa. She climbed on top of me and gave me a deep kiss, tongue and all.

"Are you drunk?" I asked.

"Ha-ha. We'll just say I am…"

Iris brushed back her hair, giving her a sultry look.

She undid her own blouse buttons, and the lace of her underwear and the valley of her breasts peeked through.

"I can't believe you're doing this to one of your employees."

"It's not like you're turning me down…"

She took my hand and brought it up to her exposed chest.

"You really are such a bad man—doing this while little Rila is sleeping in the next room."

"…I think you're much worse for still doing this while fully aware of that."

Iris was a different sort of woman than Rila was.

# 16
# Work as an Examiner

Iris had ordered me to act as the full-time proctor for any and all aspiring adventurers who came to the guild. That might've sounded like a lot, but Lahti wasn't a very large town, so we only got around two applicants per week.

Any other time, it was business as usual.

"A full-time examiner… Sounds pretty cool," Milia said, seeming excited.

I was looking at an adventurer application.

"No…I don't think it's particularly cool or anything…"

On the other side of the counter, a girl was waiting for me to administer the test.

Her name was Carolina Bethly, and she was fifteen years old. Her skill was…not great… It wasn't very versatile, and there were few situations where it'd actually be helpful. It didn't seem like she was practicing any particular sort of martial discipline, either.

The application slip I had her fill out had a cute-looking cat drawn on it. Next to the doodle were the words: *I'm counting on you!* ♪

"…"

This was giving me a headache.

"Whoa! A kitty. That's so cute," Milia commented as she peeked at the form.

Carolina didn't seem particularly interesting to me, but I had a feeling Milia would get along well with her.

There were many kinds of adventurers, but when it came to something like this, I just had no idea what to do.

"Miss Carolina Bethly."

"Oh! Yes! You can call me Lina, sir."

That nickname reminded me too much of the little mage from the party of heroes, so that was a no.

I confirmed a few outstanding points with the young woman and got verification for everything that needed it.

"Miss Carolina, if you would please take a seat, we can commence with the magic measurement."

"Okay, okay!"

Her pigtails bounced as she skipped over to the chair at the end of the counter.

We used a special crystal to measure magic. The evaluation rank was determined by the number it displayed.

"Please hold your hand over this."

"Okay, okay!"

*Just one* okay *will suffice.* I nearly vocalized the thought but thankfully stopped myself.

When Carolina held her hand over it, the light-blue crystal began to glow slightly in response.

The number it displayed was 140.

The benchmark value for what was generally considered C rank was a thousand. That meant Carolina rated very poorly. With a fluid motion, I recorded the number on her application slip. May-lee had gotten a little over six hundred. Even that had been considered fairly poor. Things didn't look good for Carolina.

"Is that it?" the girl asked.

"Yes, thank you. Next, we'll move on to the practical test."

Since Carolina had no experience with martial arts, I'd thought that perhaps she had outstanding magical aptitude to make up for it. That seemed unlikely based on her mana level.

"Um..."

"Yes, what is it?"

"Could I pass on the practical?" Carolina said slowly.

"Uhhh, it's a part of the exam."

"I don't really want to become an adventurer to fight or anything. I'm not even gonna take on any dangerous quests."

"There certainly are those who focus on herb-gathering quests. Reaching the fields where those herbs grow isn't like a walk down the street, however. If they were that easy to pick, there'd be no need to put in quests for them."

"Hmph. I guess sooo." Carolina's pigtails bounced slightly as she pouted.

She couldn't use magic, she didn't have a weapon she was proficient with, and she didn't know any hand-to-hand-combat techniques.

"Nnnnnn... I really don't think I need the practical test."

"That's an automatic failure."

"That wouldn't be good... I guess having a skill like Poison Resistance isn't all that great."

I gave no word of agreement on that.

If only she had some other talent, like magic, that really would've helped.

"Why do you want to become an adventurer?"

"I don't. It's more that I want to be an herb doctor."

...Apparently, you couldn't judge a book by its cover.

"I want to travel to all kinds of places, study flowers and medicine, and then return home as a full-fledged herbalist."

Such an aspiration was achievable without becoming an adventurer, but the value of being able to join parties and trade information with others couldn't be denied.

"I see. So this is something like a checkpoint on your way to becoming an herb doctor, then?"

"That's exactly right! ♪"

Carolina's words were grating. Maybe I just couldn't stand girls like her.

"I heard this guild passed a lot of people, so..."

*I see. She came here hoping it'd be an easy test.*

"If you end up failing, what will you do?"

"I'll just head off to the next guild. I've got no reflexes, and I can't use magic... I just need someone to help me... I'm still studying, but I know a good amount of stuff about medicine already. I was thinking I could join parties and give them advice on what curatives to use..."

She was driven. It seemed she knew her strengths and weaknesses. She'd thought this out far more than I'd first given her credit for. I was suddenly struck with curiosity about one thing she'd mentioned.

"How tolerant is your Poison Resistance skill?"

"An appraiser in the city told me that it would cut the effects of any toxin by ninety percent."

"So you'd only suffer ten percent where others would take a full one hundred?"

"Yes."

"Hmm…interesting."

"Um, how, exactly? You were laughing in your head because of how worthless a skill it is, weren't you?"

I shook my head and leveled a very serious gaze at Carolina.

"I would never do that. I think it's a lovely skill to have."

"Wha—?! Uh, um… No one's ever said that to me before…"

Carolina bashfully twirled a lock of her hair with her index finger.

"Each Adventurers Guild has its own characteristics. I suppose you could call them regional differences."

For guilds near the ocean, it was easier for adventurers proficient with swimming and diving to gather. There would undoubtedly be a lot of other quests dealing with the ocean, too.

Similarly, whether a guild operated in a cold region or a warm one, the quests they accumulated would differ accordingly.

"I will pass you—with conditions."

"All ri… Huh? Whaaaaaat?! Why?!"

"Are you familiar with the Ellen Fatinay Marsh?"

"Elefati-what? A marsh?"

Carolina tilted her head quizzically and fluttered her eyelashes.

"It lies to the southeast. It's fairly far away. It's also hot and humid. Admittedly, it isn't a very nice region, but we recently received a long-term quest to go investigate that area."

"I see... And...?"

"The region is referred to as a marsh, but it also sports an ambient poison."

"Hmm. So you're saying that's where I come in!"

Her eyes were glittering. Her skill, normally useful only under specific circumstances, was pretty much a necessity out in that swampland. She likely wouldn't find another opportunity like this.

"A normal person would end up feeling sick to their stomach. While they wouldn't die, the poison would greatly slow their investigation."

"Oh! I can handle something like that no problem!"

"The area is mostly untamed. Doubtless you'll find many poison-resistant plants, as well as novel vegetation."

"Is that the condition?"

"Yes, please take quests from any guild stationed near Ellen Fatinay. Such a place might even have need of an herb doctor like you."

"Yes, sir!"

That was how Carolina Bethly passed her exam.

"Thank you very much, sir! This was my sixth attempt, and I was about to lose hope... I'd started to think it really was impossible for me."

"Any skill will shine when used in the right way."

I taught Carolina a relatively safe travel route to the Ellen Fatinay Marsh.

"...I'm going to work super hard! And not just for myself—for you, too!"

An adventurer permit clutched in one hand, she gave me a big wave with the other as she set off on her journey.

Several years later, word got back to me that she'd made quite the name for herself.

When I'd passed her, I hadn't had the slightest idea that she would become famed for being both an herb doctor and an adventurer.

That had been the result of her own efforts. She'd used her skill to safely traverse all manner of otherwise toxic locations and research their plants.

It was quite ironic—a girl with no talent as an adventurer ended up going on more actual adventures than anyone who came by the office to pick up a quest.

# 17

# As the Demon Lord

"How are you feeling?"

The last few days, it seemed Rila hadn't been doing so hot. She'd started spending more and more time in bed.

"I feel most unwell," Rila declared. Then she promptly burrowed beneath the covers.

I wondered if a human doctor was equipped with the knowledge necessary to diagnose a demon.

"I'll make some food. You should try to eat something if you feel hungry."

Rila didn't respond. When I started to leave, she reached out from beneath the bedsheets and grabbed my hand.

"Knave…"

"What is it? Is there something you want?"

"No…that's not it…"

"Hmm?"

*Maybe…she caught a cold?* I'd heard some people say that getting sick could make you feel a bit forlorn.

"Are you feeling lonely?"

"No, that's not it, either… Well, actually…maybe a little…"

Rila slightly poked her head out from the blankets. I stroked her red hair.

"Um, so… There is something I suspect this may be…"

"What is it?"

"…No…it's fine… I may be wrong."

That was rare. Rila never minced her words.

"I want a kiss."

"All right."

Rila puckered her lips. I kissed her several times.

"If there's anything else you want to talk about, we can go over it after I come home from work."

With that, I headed off to the guild.


The day concluded without issue, and Milia and I walked home together around sunset.

"So even Miss Prima Donna gets sick. I'll make a great meal to bring the life back into her!"

"Thank you. That will help. I can make some normal dishes, but I just don't know what to make for someone who's sick."

"No problem! I'm just glad to be of help. I'm worried about her being sick, too."

A rather motivated Milia accompanied me all the way home.

…*Huh?*

Immediately, I noticed something strange.

"Miss Prima Donna? I came to make you food." Milia opened the door to the room where Rila should have been sleeping.

I didn't sense Rila's presence.

"Huh? Miss Prima Donna isn't here."

I hadn't put her in cat form. I hadn't seen her at the guild, either. Milia and I had been in town shopping, and we hadn't run into her there, either. If she had been there, I would've certainly sensed her.

I touched the blanket of the disheveled bed. It was still slightly warm. Whatever had happened, it'd happened recently.

"I'm sorry, Miss Milia. I'm going to look for Rila."

"Oh, in that case, I'll make something and leave it here! Something you can heat up and eat."

"Thank you. I don't know when we'll be back, so you don't need to wait up."

"…I see. All right!"

I ran out of the house.

*…Perhaps someone from the demon lord army realized she was alive?* I didn't sense the demon lord. That meant the collar was still working.

Searching for a member of the demon lord army didn't pose too much of a challenge.

Almost instantly, I found traces of an inhuman presence. Scales of mana were faintly all around—creating a trail for me to follow that led south.

In addition to the Duchy of Bardenhawk, where Maylee was from, Yorvensen Kingdom also resided to the south of Lahti. They were both countries that the demon lord army had laid to waste. In particular, I'd heard there were still many remnants of the demon lord army within Yorvensen Kingdom's territory.

Rila must've been discovered by some members of her forces and, whether voluntarily or not, she was traveling with them.

As soon as I entered the forest, the mana-scale trail ended.

"…"

It seemed they'd realized they couldn't escape and had hidden themselves.

…In which case, they had to be nearby.

I detected the earth, the vegetation, the trees, the wind…and something else. A human or demon usually gave off mana. Rila's collar shut that out entirely. That absence actually made it easier to tell she was nearby.

"Hey, you who took the demon lord! I know you're here. Come out."

A dark elf emerged from the underbrush.

Her silver hair was like argent rays of moonlight, and her white eyes were serpentine. Her skin was dark. The vestiges of mana I had chased after matched what this woman's body emitted.

"I was so worried something had followed me, and now I discover it was nothing but a lowly human."

"What? You're just a dark elf."

The woman gave me a sharp look. Dark elves were a subspecies that was stronger than regular elves. As a result, they'd suffered a fair amount of persecution throughout the years, but…well, that didn't matter right now.

"Is Rila…is Rileyla safe?"

"A human the likes of you has no business uttering the name of Her Majesty the demon lord!"

The demon lord army was no longer a unified body. I'd been worried that a large group had come to take back the demon lord. That it was only one person came as a relief. Rila apparently had very loyal adherents.

"I want you to return Rila. Or is this what she wants?"

"Who do you think you're speaking to, human? I do not intend to make deals with you."

"I'll say it again: I want you to return Rila. That's my only request. If this is her will, then I want to know the reason behind it."

"The matter is already settled!"

*A female dark elf who hasn't been reported dead, who's also a loyal member of the demon lord army. That can only make her...*

First Magic Regimental Commander Roje Sandsong, a member of Rila's imperial guard.

I could kill her instantly and take Rila home, but if I didn't figure out what was going on, others from Roje's group could attempt the same feat.

Had the fake corpse that Rila created and claimed was flawless been exposed? Or had the dark elf come here simply after hearing rumors there was a demon woman in Lahti?

"I'm in a hurry. I will kill you and take Her Majesty the demon lord home."

The mana that had been flying about suddenly exploded outward and filled the area like steam.

I watched with my arms still folded.

"I will at least thank you for sheltering Her Majesty the demon lord."

"You're quite welcome."

Even if I couldn't see Roje because of how dark it was, I could tell that a vein was throbbing on her temple. It seemed she couldn't stand having a human treat her like an equal.

"You, a human, dare act so high and mighty...?! I will kill you!"

Roje Sandsong was without question one of the stronger members of Rila's army.

Unsurprisingly, her magical abilities were quite advanced. She instantly shot out offensive magic that made use of the darkness. It was a dark magic attack spell called Shadow Edge. I only barely evaded it.

A large tree behind me was cut clean through and crashed to the ground.

Roje loosed that same spell again and again.

"Just because you dodged it once—!"

As I evaded each one, I drew closer and closer.

Among all the demon lord's forces, this woman was the strongest rear guard. She was an equally capable vanguard, however, which made her troublesome. She had a Shadow Edge spell manifested in either hand as a weapon.

One was short, and one was long.

Roje was very knowledgeable about how to fight in the dark. Her blades may as well have been invisible.

"I'll have your head!"

"You should be more worried about your back."

"Hmph. A classic technique. There's nothing behind me! Seems like an improvised, human trick!"

"Scree-scree!" cried two small black shadows as they jumped at Roje from behind.

*THUNK!*

The two little things kicked Roje hard in the back of her head.

"Guh?! What was that?! ...Shadows...?!"

"Yes. They're my adorable shadows."

"When did you…?! Why would a human such as you know court-order-rank tetra magic?!"

"Rila taught me."

"…What did you say…?! But even I couldn't manage that spell…"

"So you're not even on the level of a human like me."

"Why, you…! I'll kill you!"

I summoned a few more shadows, twelve in all.

"There are so many…! Six is supposed to be the limit…"

"Is it?"

*Fwom, vwoooo, vwooom.* Roje fought back my minions with her two Shadow Edges.

*Hop, hup, floop. Floop. Tumble. Roll, roll.*

Despite her best efforts, she couldn't hit a single one.

"How are they moving like that? It's almost like they're alive!"

"I'm controlling all of them."

"Stop screwing with me! Just look at how many there are! No one but the demon lord would be able to manage such a thing!"

They weren't doing much in the way of actually hurting Roje, but I had the assistants she wasn't targeting aim some low kicks at her feet.

"Damn it!"

*Vwoooooooom!* A Shadow Edge swept low across the ground.

"Screeeee!" My little servants scattered like baby spiders.

"How infuriating…," Roje muttered. She'd completely forgotten what it was like dealing with me.

"Hey."

Realizing she'd made a huge mistake, Roje turned her gaze back to me. I flicked her forehead.

*BWOOOOOOM!* A noise like an explosion erupted as Roje was sent flying backward.

"Ngh!"

The dark elf came to an immediate stop after impacting on a large tree trunk. She slumped forward slightly, and her head sagged.

I could feel that Rila was nearby, but she said nothing. She was probably either in a state where she couldn't speak or she was unconscious. The first order of business was to find her; then I could ask her what'd happened.

Roje had proved unwilling to provide aught of use, so I decided to leave her for later.

"*Real Nightmare…* You're a dog, and I'm your owner."

"…Nnnn…ngh. Nnh. Woof?"

"There, there. Who's a good girl?"

"Wuff, wuff, wuff?"

While I patted her head, Roje happily wiggled her butt in place of a tail.

I found Rila lying on her side, hidden in some undergrowth. As I'd suspected, she was unconscious.

"Hey, Rila, wake up. What happened? Hey."

*Slap, slap, slap, slap.* I hit her face, but she didn't stir.

"…Did Roje Sandsong do something to you…?"

The dark elf was currently running in circles as she barked and tried to chase her own butt.

I didn't need her help anyway. Rila had already taught me the exact spell I needed for this.

*"Dispell."*

I hadn't used it since I'd cast it on Maylee, but it worked exactly as intended. A shattering sound filled the air.

"Rila, wake up."

"…Uh…ugh…"

Rila's eyes opened, though only just barely.

"Knave…? Oh, right. Roje had…"

"I used Dispell. What happened?"

Rila looked around and took in the situation.

"My adored subject told me she had a favor to ask. I was reluctant but agreed to meet her here anyway. When I told her that I was not feeling well, she cast Sleep magic to put me under and make the journey more comfortable."

"A favor?"

"Yes… I think it would do well for her to explain it all herself."

"Wuff, woof, guuuuuuh, wuff?"

The dark elf, who was on all fours, happily ran to my side when beckoned.

"Real Nightmare, I see… This is quite a sight, but I cannot bear to watch my adored subject barking like a dog," Rila said.

Since I couldn't get the dark elf to explain things while in dog mode, I broke the spell.

I clapped my hands in front of Roje's face.

"—Huh?! Why was I acting like a mongrel…?!"

"Was playing dog fun?"

"You…! You dare use a makeshift Real Nightmare on me?! I'll kill you!"

Before the dark elf could do anything, however, Rila stopped her. "Wait, Roje. I will not allow you to lay a hand on him. This man is my partner."

"…Huh? What…are you saying, Great Demon Lord? I do not quite understand the meaning of the word…*p-partner*? *Partner??*"

"You may try to lay a hand on him, but he is not an opponent you would want to face. It would be all you could do just to survive."

"Tch… Do you mean that?" Roje pierced me with a sharp look.

"He is so powerful that I was defeated in less than thirty minutes."

"Y-you couldn't even match him for a half hour, Great Demon Lord…? Impossible…!"

Roje was taken aback, but I had to correct Rila. I had certainly won in under thirty minutes, but there was a more accurate measurement.

"You gave in less than ten minutes after we started the battle," I amended.

"Wait, it happened in even less time?!"

"Ahem." Rila cleared her throat. "Regardless, I acknowledged this man's prowess and offered him everything…and made him a vow…"

"Great Demon Lord… This is the first time I've ever seen you act so womanly…"

"And in another type of first tussle, she didn't even last five minutes and immediately—"

"S-stop that. D-d-do not speak of such things before one of my subjects."

Rila hid her face behind her hands, and her ears turned red. Evidently, she was recalling our first time.

"...Great Demon Lord, you seem bashful enough to die... I've never seen you act this way before..." Roje beheld Rila with a dead expression. She quickly recovered, however, shaking her head and pointing at me. "That doesn't mean I have to accept you, though!" she declared.

"I don't care. Let's get back on topic. Roje Sandsong, why did you try to take Rila?"

Roje glanced at Rila, who nodded slightly.

"I will start from the beginning. I sensed that Her Majesty the demon lord was in battle and quickly headed back to her audience chambers, where I found her corpse lying in the hall."

"Roje, I am impressed you discovered it was a fake. That duplicate was created using some of the highest techniques at my disposal. How did you figure it out?"

"That false corpse lacked something that only one such as I, who has bathed with you before, could know of."

"What would that be...?"

Roje nodded. "The mark on your buttocks."

"Ha-ha-ha, you fool! I have nothing of the sort!"

"Actually, you do."

"You most assuredly do."

"......"

"I will continue. In any case, I knew that you had survived. I surmised you must have been faced with some unavoidable situation that could only have been solved by faking your death and fleeing the castle."

Somewhat ignoring the explanation, Rila was practically bending over backward in an attempt to check her own butt. I continued to listen intently.

Roje, loyal subject that she was, had assumed there to be some secret reason behind the fake corpse. As such, she hadn't mentioned it to anyone else. In the months that'd followed the end of the war, she'd never given up hope that her master was still alive somewhere. In time, devout members of the demon lord army had started proposing they resume their campaign against human nations.

"Word that our charismatic and magnificent demon lord had perished was a heavy blow to many. There were those among our forces who temporarily withdrew."

*I see.* While the demon lord had died, her influence had not. My old party was able to break into the demon lord's castle because her primary forces were busy battling the allied human armies.

"The ninth division commander, Corniel Vazuli, as well as other devotees, used a quest for vengeance as an excuse to start a campaign to reclaim your castle."

"Hmm... So if my death is a reason to resume the war..."

"If we reveal you still are alive, the die hards will lose their cause. I dare not admit it in front of them, but as part of the moderate faction, I think that retreat came at the best possible time..."

Many on the human side had been exhausted. The war had become a mire. It seemed the same had applied to the demon lord army.

"Corniel is gathering those demons still hiding on the continent. With a sizable enough force, they'll retake the demon lord's castle."

Demons as a species had originally lived on another continent called Hell. They'd used a large-scale type of teleportation magic in order to come to this continent.

One of the two countries they had ravaged, Yorvensen Kingdom, had been invaded and brought under their rule. The demon lord's castle that Corniel's group was after was actually Yorvensen Kingdom's castle. In order to get a foothold within Yorvensen Kingdom, the demons had also invaded Maylee's homeland, the Duchy of Bardenhawk.

After realizing how severe a threat the demons posed, the seven kings—King Randolf included—had held meetings to form an allied force.

Yorvensen Kingdom was still a dangerous area where monsters and demons prowled. The hero party hadn't invaded Hell to defeat the demon lord but had actually only recaptured a human nation.

"Rila, they might not stop even if you reveal that you survived," I cautioned.

"I know that...but they should at least lend their demon lord an ear."

There was some truth in that, but...

"The war we waged was wrong... I learned what *warmth* is from living with you. I learned what a hallowed thing a *normal way of life* is by sharing one with you… That alone, however, is likely not enough for me to repent. So, in order to atone, I have decided I will go with Roje. I suppose you could say it's my final duty as the demon lord."

*I see. I think I understand things now.*

"In that case, while I may not be able to provide much, I'll do all in my power to aid you," I said.

"…Are you sure? If I reveal that I have survived, the humans will not remain ignorant of it forever. Your false report will come to light. Human armies may again rise to kill me… If that happens, I will…"

"I 'killed' the demon lord. I do not fail in my work. If they intend to kill Rila the individual, I'll take on a division, a whole army, or even a nation."

Rila embraced me with tears in her eyes. I held her close and stroked her head.

"My eyes did not deceive me," Rila said.

"Damn it… This human…is kind of cool…"

While we were on the move, Roje filled us in on the particulars.

"When news of Her Majesty the demon lord's death reached them, many of the moderates immediately used the Gate teleportation spell and returned to our home country. As I knew of your secret survival and the unrest of the devotees, I pretended to be one myself and remained on this continent."

Rila told me that Gate was court-order-rank penta transportation magic.

"The only one capable of teleporting the entire army is Her Majesty the demon lord herself. There are many who can teleport twenty or thirty strong, however."

Apparently, those who'd remained behind were recruiting their own on an island off the coast of the former Yorvensen Kingdom at that very moment. At the former demon lord's castle, a portion of the allied forces that had renamed themselves the Public Order Corps were driving back the monsters and demons who had encroached upon the area.

"As far as I am aware, the devotees on the island soon plan to command troops for transport in order to take back the demon lord's castle."

"It would be irksome should they teleport."

"Precisely."

When battling the demon lord army, the most troubling thing had been their teleportation magic.

Despite the enemy possessing fewer numbers, their surprise attacks could appear literally anywhere—something that had caused quite a bit of chaos.

"Rila, is there a way to prevent a jump?"

"There is. A Gate cannot simply take you anywhere. It requires a path to be connected between an entrance and an exit."

"So we just need to destroy the exit, then?"

When I said that, Roje added, "The island is only a few miles off the shore. If they realize they cannot use a Gate, they will likely cross the sea on monsters."

That being the case, taking Rila to the island in an attempt to stop the attack before it happened seemed like a better idea.

"The Gate that I created is just ahead. If we can get there, we can jump to the island."

Roje had intentionally placed the Gate a good distance from my house so as not to arouse any suspicion.

"The forces on the island number at around two thousand— monsters included. There are still demons who hide on the continent waiting for an opportune moment, though," Roje told us.

The demon lord's castle was symbolic to Rila's forces. If it fell into the hands of demons again, word would spread quickly and inspire even more demons and monsters to converge upon it.

"Over there." Roje pointed at a hut. When we reached it, she led us around behind it. There I could detect several traces of mana.

"Th-that's odd... What?!" Roje exclaimed.

"What's wrong?" I asked.

"It seems that the Gate Roje set up has been destroyed," said Rila.

Before we even had time to ask who'd done it, someone appeared on a hill that overlooked the hut.

"I thought that something was up... Lord Roje, what are you doing consorting with a human in a place like this?"

The speaker looked to be a small boy. He was sitting down with a grin on his face and his chin propped on both his hands.

"Delacress...! So you destroyed my Gate!"

"C'mon—tell me what you were doing."

Roje was speechless, but Rila spoke up in her place. "Delacress Berobea! It is I!"

"…Great…Demon Lord…?"

Delacress's forehead creased as he narrowed his eyes.

"I have been informed of the situation. I would like a conference with the ninth division commander, Corniel Vazuli."

"There is no Great Demon Lord anymore."

"That was a fake corpse and, as you can see, I am still in good health."

"I don't really care who you are. Just don't get in our way."

"Listen to reason, Delacress! She is undeniably the true Great Demon Lord!"

Refusing to listen, Delacress got to his feet.

*If I'm not mistaken, this kid is…*

"Even you can't stand up to me, Lady Roje." Delacress suddenly began emitting a huge amount of mana. His body, small like a child's, started to glow. *"Dragorize."*

*Delacress Berobea…*

He was a special-maneuver battalion commander in the demon lord army and a dragonkin. His role primarily consisted of air raids and leading the monsters in battle.

*"Groooaaarrrrrr!"*

A dark dragon appeared before our very eyes.

"Delacress, you little…! You've been watching my every move, haven't you…?!" cried Roje.

"Delacress! Please listen to what I have to say—!" Rila implored.

As the dragon opened his gigantic maw, his chest swelled.

"Hey, Roje Sandsong, he's going to use a breath attack. Can you put up a defense against that?" I asked.

"Just once, if I put all my mana into it! I won't be able to perform a jump after that, though."

"Good enough. I'll leave protecting the deadweight to you."

"Grrr... I have no rebuke...," Rila replied.

"You! You called Her Majesty the demon lord *deadweight*! Take that back! Correct yourself and repent immediately!" Roje was livid, and anger was plain in her eyes.

"It's coming."

"You act all high and mighty! I doubt that the likes of a human could do anything to Delacress after he's cast Dragorize! Hmph. Even a wild dragon would avert its eyes and tuck its tail beneath its legs at such a sight! Understand? So get ready to apologi— Huh? Where'd you go?"

"Roje, I can hardly tell whose side you are on anymore," Rila said.

A unique magic circle appeared in the dragon's mouth. A gigantic gout of dark fire began to pour from the jagged maw.

*"Grrroooaaawww!"*

The dragon breathed. Roje had said she could guard against one such attack, so I didn't pay her and Rila much mind as I headed out of range. Just as the dark elf had claimed, she really could defend against the breath attack.

The thing that made dragons trouble was how durable their scales were. A normal blade could not hope to penetrate their skin. Complicating things was a personal rule of mine: I never carried a special weapon with me.

At the same time, since dragon hide contained anti-magic properties, any half-baked magic attack wouldn't work on them, either. Naturally, my entire repertoire consisted of half-baked spells. If I had magical abilities that would work on a dragon, I likely wouldn't have become an assassin.

I invoked my skill. Just to be sure, I erased any trace of my presence using Unobtrusive.

I didn't know if the same held true for dragonkin, but wild dragons were incredibly sensitive to mana.

Unobtrusive was the ideal skill for a feint. You would just fire off magic at will and activate the skill at the moment the spell hit. By doing that, the enemy would have no idea from where they were being attacked. During that opening, the main force—Almelia or Lina—would strike. Such a diversion worked only when those two heavy hitters were around, however.

This time, I couldn't expect something like that.

"Tch! What is that human doing?! He's not any use at all! Has he run away?!"

Delacress inhaled in preparation for another attack.

That was the moment I'd been waiting for. Gripping his scales with my arms and legs, I moved along Delacress's neck, quickly reaching his face.

"Dragons are certainly regarded as the most powerful of creatures. Clumsy physical and magical attacks can't hurt them. Their flight and breath attacks make them veritable flying fortresses."

"When did he get up there?! H-how did he get that close to a dragon when they're so sensitive to mana? Wh-what is he intending to do...?"

Delacress noticed me, and his eyes pivoted.

Just like the first time, a magic circle had appeared in his mouth, and dark flames were starting to gather.

A dragon's breath was a type of magic where a dense amount of mana went through a special magic circle as the dragon exhaled.

"I wonder what'd happen if I was to use a Match spell right now. Sure, it's the weakest of fire magics and only used for everyday living, but let's find out…"

With a miniscule amount of mana, I ignited a small flame on my fingertip.

The dragon's eyes filled with fear.

He tried to close his mouth, but he was too late. With a snap, I flicked the small bit of fire into the dragon's jaws.

Magic circles are a kind of formula. If they possess any special characteristics, it gives them a sort of fragility. A dragon's breath, in particular, utilizes a unique sort of magical array. If one suffered any sort of outside influence, like a foreign bit of mana or a spell…

"It'll easily explode."

A brilliant light began to spill from the dragon's mouth.

The next moment, there came a terrific detonation that seemed to shake the very air.

"Graaaghhh…"

The dragon's eyes rolled back as he fell. His neck thudded limply on the ground. His transformation immediately melted away, and Delacress returned to his child body. Faced with a dragon about to breathe fire, most would try to run, defend, or otherwise make their peace with death. Doubtless, there weren't many who'd think to launch their own spell back at the magic-resistant creature—especially at its mouth.

"You took down Delacress in dragon form…with such a small flame…," Roje muttered, overcome with shock.

◆

I returned to the two women.

Rila and Roje talked over what we would be doing next.

"Great Demon Lord, we can no longer jump to the island. I lack the proper amount of mana… So I think we will need to find a place that will provision us with horses and then locate a ship of some sort…"

"No, we likely do not need that."

"But…we have no method of transport."

Rila shook her head at Roje's perplexed expression.

I already knew what Rila was up to.

"What say you, knave? Do you think you will be able to learn court-order-rank penta transportation magic?"

"If it's less complex than Shadow, I don't think it'll be a problem."

"…Huh? You scoundrel! You dare look down upon Gate magic?! You may have learned Shadow, but demon magic is not that easy! If you make a mistake with the arrival coordinates, you will forever be trapped in subspace."

"What if I used the Gate that Roje Sandsong set up near the demon lord's castle as the exit point?"

"That sounds like an excellent idea. Get to it."

"Are you even listening to me?!"

I ignored Roje's screeching as I cast Gate precisely how Rila had shown me.

A magic circle about the width of one's shoulders appeared on the ground.

This was the entrance. We were using the entrance that Roje had established on the island as our exit. I found Roje's mana through the magic circle immediately.

"I've located the entrance Roje Sandsong set up. I will connect the path."

No sooner had I thought I'd done it than the magic circle on the ground began glowing.

"Hmm. Hmm. Mm-hmm... Looks like you've connected a path that runs about one hundred and twenty-five miles to the south," Rila said as she looked at the magic circle.

"That's a considerable distance. That puts it in the Yorvensen Kingdom. Is it safe to say this is a success, then?" I asked.

Rila grinned.

"It is."

Roje fell to her knees. "I hate this. What is with this human...? I endured so much hardship just to learn Gate magic..."

"This man's magic sensibilities are incredibly high, so much so that they dwarf even that of demons. Do not be so glum."

"Great Demon Lord...your words of solace warm my heart so..."

Roje seemed touched by Rila's consideration.

"Well then, we best make the jump."

Rila held my hand. Roje took Rila's other hand, as well as my own, forming a circle. All the magic circle needed to activate was my standing on it. I tested it out. For a moment, a sense of weight-lessness enveloped my whole body.

I barely had time to feel anything, but in the blink of an eye, my entire surroundings had changed. There was a beach only a short distance away.

"It appears the jump was a success."

"Hmph! Seems you've received praise from Her Majesty the demon lord herself. Accept that with gratitude, you pitiful human."

Roje was like a squeaky third wheel.

Anyway, we had arrived behind a large rock on the island where those remaining demons devoted to restarting the war had holed up.

"This is Corniel's territory. We must be cautious of making any movements that attract attention."

Roje looked at me as she said that.

*That's what I specialize in, though…*

"You said that they had about two thousand, didn't you? Doesn't that mean that we just need to kill them all?"

"Ah-ha-ha-ha-ha, are you saying you can do that by yourself? I'd like to see you try!"

"Roje, stop. He'll actually do it. Roland wouldn't propose some-thing like that on a whim or to put on airs."

Roje tilted her head quizzically as her eyes went wide. "But, Great Demon Lord…is this man not a mage…?"

She likely had made that misconception because she hadn't seen me use any assassination techniques. There was no point in going out of my way to demonstrate them, after all.

"Knave, I would like you to take me to Corniel."

"But, Rila—"

"Say no more," Rila interrupted, silencing me. "No matter what kind of subjects they are, I do not wish for anyone else to die."

"Great Demon Lord...I will follow you wherever you go...! I will also help you persuade Lord Corniel to stop!"

"..."

Roje led the way around the island.

A watchtower had been erected on a point of slight elevation. It was most likely used to spot any approaching enemies. None of them had thought to suspect an enemy arriving by teleportation, however.

"That's odd... There are no lookouts. Even before dawn, someone is usually on duty."

*"RAAAAHHHHHHH!"*

A thundering war cry shook the ground beneath us.

"It couldn't be... Are they doing it today—?"

"Roje, what's wrong?"

"Great Demon Lord, I apologize. It seems that they had not informed me of the appointed day..."

"That dragonkin followed you. They probably didn't trust you."

"Tsk... It seems you're right... But we still made it in time! Let us make haste, Great Demon Lord. The center of the island is an open field, and I believe that is where that cry came from. Based on their activity, I believe they have finished creating a Gate near the former demon lord's castle." Roje went into a sprint as she continued. "Great Demon Lord, there are military physicians on the island. It may be prudent to seek their examination."

"If there are any here, we shall inquire about that once this matter is settled."

The three of us hurried up a hill.

Below us was the center of the island. We could see a group of demons and monsters that was large enough to blot out a small field.

Just as Roje had said, there were quite a few of them.

"The demon lord shall be avenged, and we shall retake her castle! This is our time to show our might to those cowards who ran home with their tails between their legs—!"

A demon was addressing the assembled troops to boost their morale.

""*GRAAAHHHHHH!*"" came another war cry.

If those forces teleported one after another, they did have a chance at taking back the demon lord's castle rather easily. If that happened, it would surely spark another war with humanity, though likely a smaller one.

My presence would throw a wrench into things, so I hid in the shadows of the rocks and resigned myself to watch.

"All of you!"

Rila's cry brought silence and then a great commotion.

"G-Great Demon Lord…?"

"But she was defeated by the hero!"

Rila put up a hand to silence the troops. Looking upon her in that moment reminded me once again that she really was the demon lord.

"That the demon lord Rileyla Diakitep passed on was a falsehood. As you see, I am very much alive, my brethren!"

""HRAAAHHHHHH!""

A cheer far louder than any heard previously rang out.

It seemed Roje hadn't been wrong when she'd called Rila *charismatic*.

"Enough is enough. We lost the battle. Brethren, we must go back to Hell. You are not bound for human lands; you must return to our home."

A stir ran through the crowd.

"What is going on…?"

"Great Demon Lord…?"

"Has the ruthless, merciless great demon lord really acknowledged defeat…?"

Cutting through the disarray, the demon who'd earlier been addressing the army spoke up. He was Corniel Vazuli, the ninth division commander. He was well known as the most war-hungry man in the demon lord army.

"Quiet, you lot! …Her Majesty the demon lord would not say such a thing! Just look for yourselves! Does this so-called great demon lord have the mana to go with the title? I certainly don't think so!"

I watched Corniel's face and saw that he looked surprised to see Rila, but maybe she didn't matter to him anymore. His claims of a noble quest for revenge were clearly an empty excuse for violence. Even the real demon lord couldn't stop him now.

"That's right… Her Majesty the demon lord would never accept defeat!"

"There is no way Her Majesty the demon lord wouldn't have any mana!"

"That's right! That's right!"

Roje protested, but it was to little avail.

"Too bad, Roje Sandsong." Corniel sneered.

"Damn it…!"

"I knew you were sniffing about doing something in secret. I suppose this is what you were working toward."

"…"

"We are the demon lord army! We will reclaim the demon lord's castle and then head north! The human lands shall be ours again!"

Rila paled. "You plan to march north of the castle?"

If the capital of the former Yorvensen Kingdom was to fall to demons once again, the neighboring former Duchy of Bardenhawk would not go unscathed.

…Most dire of all, *she* was there.

"Y-you must not do this!" Rila pleaded.

"Who are the prized and most powerful warriors of the demon lord army? Let me hear it!"

*YAH! YAH! YAH! YAH!*

The demons were too fired up. It was clear they weren't going to listen to Rila anymore. Such had been the same for that dragonkin.

…They were going to attack.

Even if the small army knew how outnumbered they were, they seemed incapable of refusing the call to war.

"G-Great Demon Lord…"

"L-listen! Listen to what I have to say! Why are you going to such lengths to fight?!" Rila had said previously that she didn't want anyone to die, but a new determination could be seen in her eyes now. "I no longer possess any mana because I have acquired knowledge of the world's most powerful skill!"

*What the hell is she talking about?*

Clearly, everyone else was thinking the same sort of thing.

The crowd quieted as they listened for what Rila would say next.

"Of all the things you could blurt out! Absurd!"

"Corniel, run along home to Hell. This is my final warning."

"How you make me laugh! I will rebuild the demon lord army and crush every human nation beneath my heel!"

"You always were a complete fool… It's why I could never rely on you…"

Rila's eyes narrowed in an expression of sadness. At the same time, however, she was looking to where I'd hidden myself. I met her gaze.

*I understand…*

"I will kill you without moving an inch by using the one and only Instant Death skill!"

"I should like to see you try, Great Demon Lord—or should I say, impostor?!"

"Farewell, Corniel… Die."

The moment the words left Rila's lips, I leaped out from my hiding spot behind the rocks at top speed.

I activated Unobtrusive.
*Rila, I will not let your resolve or your bluff go to waste.*

*Acting as her Instant Death, I will assassinate this demon right before their very eyes.*

Unaware of my approach, Corniel broke into a laugh.

"What's an Instant Death skill supposed to even be?! Ha-ha-ha-ha! Are you planning on making me laugh to death?! Ha-ha-ha-ha—ha… Gah…?!"

Drawing Corniel's own sword with a backhanded grip, I thrust it straight through his chest.

With a force of two thousand present, it was likely that at least a few of the demons had access to healing magic. That posed a problem. I had to make sure Corniel died immediately.

Lifting the demon man's reserve sword off his hip, I plunged that into his chest as well. Corniel was also wearing a gaudily decorated dagger. I used that to quickly stab him twice in the neck. The goal was to sever his major arteries. I was confident he would die instantly from this.

I felt my skill's effect expiring, and so I leaped to the other side of the hill. It was a blind spot where the crowd wouldn't find me. When I finally stopped running, my ears caught panicked shrieks.

"What was that just now?!"

"When did a sword get into his chest—?!"

"L-Lord Cornieeeeeeeeeeeeeel?!"

"Sh-she's not faking. Only the real demon lord could've done that!"

"I-it's got to be her! She must have developed that terrifying Instant Death magic in exchange for her mana…!"

Rila once again raised her voice to address the startled crowd.

"Heed my words!! Should you not, you shall know the same fate!"

After that Instant Death performance, Rila had the army shivering in their boots. They hung on her every word.

Roje took command and issued orders for the troops to return to Hell.

"I am impressed that you realized what I was thinking," Rila said to me as she giggled under her breath like a child who'd pulled a prank.

"It was obvious after you made up that unbelievable Instant-Death-skill story. You also looked right at me. I got the meaning."

"Ha-ha. You yourself *are* my Instant Death skill. However, that was quite a feat. You did indeed bring death to Corniel in an instant," Rila said with satisfaction. At the base of the hill, she watched her subjects teleport back to Hell one after another.

"Roje mentioned there were some physicians on the island. They'll end up going home at this rate. Are you sure you shouldn't look for them?" I asked.

"There's one in the barracks who is to remain here a bit longer. I will have them examine me later."

While Rila had complained a few times about not feeling well, she looked fine to me.

"Don't push yourself. I understand wounds to a certain extent, but illnesses are a separate matter. Especially so because you're a demon."

"I know that. I know... Ha-ha. You seem quite worried about me."

Rila happily entwined her arms around me.

"Well then, let's go to the barracks and see the doctor," I declared.

"I—I will be doing that alone. Don't follow me!"

*What's got her so angry?*

Rila insisted that I was not to follow. Suddenly presented with nothing to do, I absentmindedly watched the rest of the army march into the teleportation circle.

"Hey, human. Where is Her Majesty the demon lord?" Roje inquired.

"Your resplendent leader is meeting with a doctor in the barracks. She told me not to follow her, so I don't recommend going to see her right now."

"Ha-ha-ha. The trust between Her Majesty the demon lord and I, her first magic regimental commander, is far beyond the likes of you, human. I have sworn an oath of everlasting fealty to her. Don't compare yourself to me."

Roje smiled haughtily and began recounting various stories about her time serving under Rila.

"Is this going to be long?" I asked.

"You may have shared some time with her, but that's nothing compared to my acquaintance with Her Majesty. She and I have even bathed together."

That wasn't such a big deal. I'd done that, too... Rila and I bathed together about four times a week.

Actually, it wasn't that we planned to wash together. More often than not, Rila simply joined me in the tub after I'd already gotten in.

*"I-it is more efficient if we take one together...since the water will get cold. Yes, that's it...,"* Rila would say without waiting to hear my answer.

"Her Majesty the demon lord is just as impressive as ever. I never would've guessed that her loss of mana was the price for having developed a frighteningly powerful new skill." Roje nodded, deeply moved. "A power that brings death with but a single word. You must make sure not to get on Her Majesty the demon lord's bad side, human. Either way, I'm sure she'll tell you to die someday, and you'll have no choice but to do it."

"You realize you're talking to the Instant Death skill himself, right?"

"Huh?"

I shook my head. "Never mind. Why are you so loyal to Rila anyway? You're an elf, aren't you? You're not a demon."

"Human, do you realize how the demon lord is chosen?" Roje asked.

"All I know is that it's not an inherited title."

"Usually that is the case, yes. Her Majesty the demon lord is the child of the former demon lord, however. In her youth, she continually astounded those around her with her overwhelming wit. There were none who dared to oppose her ascendancy to demon lord."

Despite it not being a hereditary title, a demon lord's child had become the next demon lord. I didn't know how demon society operated, but I couldn't imagine such an upset being much fun for someone else who'd been seeking the throne.

"There is no one who has done more for the sake of demons or Hell than Her Majesty the demon lord herself. She even cares for her servants. There are many who would do anything for her."

I suddenly remembered something that'd been on my mind since Rila had first been kidnapped by Roje.

"Roje Sandsong...whose orders are you following?"

At first I'd assumed the dark elf had acted of her own accord, but this seemed too big an affair for that. Someone else had to have directed her here and given her a mission.

"You...are sharp." Roje chuckled.

"If you really were just a moderate, you would've gone home to Hell. Hearing that the devotees died gallant deaths would've been comfort enough. I doubt you'd weep over any human casualties."

What's more, Roje had gone out of her way to search for the missing Rila. It suggested there was something Roje needed to explain to the demon lord.

"What's your aim?" I pressed.

"Nothing quite so sinister. The grand lord, Her Majesty the demon lord's father, is retired from active duty, but he is still in good health. After we lost the war, the grand lord told me to watch over those demons who'd remained in human territory while also searching for the 'dead' demon lord."

Roje could use Gate magic. She had likely infiltrated the devo-tees while informing the grand lord of their movements.

"I said I hadn't told anyone about Her Majesty the demon lord's survival, but that was a lie. I did inform the grand lord of it."

Corniel and his forces had gone rogue. As their counterattack drew nearer, Roje caught wind of a woman living in a human town who was rumored to be a demon.

"The word was that this demon was an unrivaled beauty. I knew it had to be Her Majesty the demon lord. The grand lord told me that, '*Rileyla will surely stop Corniel after learning of the ensuing revolt. You shall be the one to tell her.*'"

It seemed the grand lord did not wish for the devotees to die in vain.

"Her Majesty the demon lord inherited from her father the con-cern she shows to her subjects. That is why Her Majesty the demon lord made her way here in order to stop them. I must admit, I didn't expect her to have no mana at her disposal, though," Roje admitted. "In exchange for that, however, she brought along a man who's proven to be incredibly reliable... N-not that I personally think that! It's just that Her Majesty the demon lord does! Don't get the wrong idea!"

I hadn't said anything, but Roje was wagging her finger and seemingly scolding me.

"All right, all right," I said while shrugging.

Before long, the entirety of the army was gone, and the clearing at the bottom of the hill was empty.

Rila was taking a long time to get back, so Roje and I headed to the barracks to investigate. The building itself looked like it'd been hastily built using earth magic.

"You wait here, you scoundrel!" Roje ordered bluntly when we arrived at the entrance.

No sooner had she done so than a stooped old woman no taller than a child emerged from inside.

"Hmm? My esteemed physician, how is Her Majesty the demon lord?"

"Roje, is it? Good job. It's still hard to believe that Lady Rileyla has indeed returned, however..."

The old woman, who smiled bitterly, sat down on a stump, pulled out a pipe, and began to smoke. Based on how she was acting, Rila didn't seem to be suffering from anything serious.

She told us that Rila was in the medical room, and Roje immediately led me there.

"Hey, Rila, how're you doing?"

"Your Majesty...how are you faring?"

Rila was lying faceup on the bed. She turned away from me.

"Mm...not...bad."

"What did the physician say, Your Majesty...?"

"Hmm..."

Rila glanced at me, averted her gaze, and immediately turned red.

"Your Majesty, are you embarrassed...?"

Roje's nose was bleeding, and she looked close to swooning.

"I wonder if I say this...whether you will come to hate me or not..."

Rila wriggled and spoke in a way that was unlike her.

"I would never hate you!" Roje declared.

"I'm not asking you."

"Understood!"

Since Rila apparently wanted to be alone with me, Roje was shooed out of the examination room. She looked terribly unhappy.

"I cannot speak of such things in front of my subjects…"

"So what happened?" I asked.

Rila, now red to the tips of her ears, averted her gaze and muttered, "Like I said, it…actually… And that's how it is…"

Even sitting on the bed with my ear turned toward Rila, her words were still unintelligible.

"Rila, I can't hear what you're saying. Please speak clearly. Is it something serious?"

"N-no…"

She didn't seem to want to say it. Groaning and blushing, she turned to look at me.

"Like I said, it's…"

"Mm-hmm."

"I worked hard cooking something two days ago, did I not? I sampled it several times as I experimented…but it wound up being no good. In more ways than one."

"What were you doing? …That's silly."

"S-stop that! A-as I said, I did not want to say anything."

As though to hide her embarrassment, Rila smacked me.

Roje was eavesdropping from a gap in the door and whispered to herself, "You made yourself ill with your own cooking… How terribly clumsy… You're so cute, Your Majesty—the cutest demon lord to have ever lived."

◆

There was little else for me to do but sigh at Rila's considerable clumsiness.

"I'm glad nothing serious happened," I said.

"Actually, it happened during dinner two days ago," Rila admitted.

"I see. I was fine, though."

"...That's ridiculous. You partook of the same food... Did I prepare something that somehow only nauseated demons?"

"I doubt it. Part of my training involved building up a tolerance to poisons. That's probably all it was."

"Of course! That is quite the relief."

After enjoying a hearty laugh, Rila suddenly turned so serious, she was practically shaking.

"...How dare you call my food *poison*...!"

"It had all the necessary nutrients, so I had no complaints, but it's fortunate I'd undergone training. If I hadn't, I likely would've died."

I was glad Rila hadn't made that deadly dish during the party we'd had with Milia and Iris.

Rila punched me in the gut.

"Ouch?!"

She succeeded only in hurting her own fist, however.

"So that's why you were worried I would hate you?" I asked.

Rila nodded. "...I am not entirely perfect... I will likely continue to make unforeseen errors when preparing meals in the future."

Over the past few weeks that we'd spent together, it'd become fairly obvious that Rila was cooking via a trial-and-error method. Whenever she went into town to buy ingredients, she would ask the very same merchants she bought from how to cook. Rila no doubt assumed I wasn't aware, but it was obvious. Especially because she'd been writing notes for herself.

Unfortunately, even those drafted instructions had failed to yield palatable results.

At first, Rila had said she cooked only to pass the time. As I thought about it, I realized that she'd recently taken to asking for my thoughts on her cooking a lot more, however.

So when it came to all her hard work…

"You don't need to worry about me. Feel free to keep cooking."

Rila's expression conveyed that she understood. She brought her face closer, and our lips touched. As though she was begging for more, Rila wrapped her arms around my neck.

"Wha…? What…?"

Roje was still peeking in on us from the entrance to the room. Her eyes seemed robbed of all life, but her teeth were chattering.

"That human compared Her Majesty the demon lord's cooking to poison…and even took her in his arms and genuinely kissed her… Why? How? This is inconceivable. How could Her Majesty—the rose of Hell—the woman who used her charisma, beauty, and wit to command the demon lord army—fall in with such a lowly creature? Unbelievable, unbelievable, unbelieveableunbelieveableunbelieveableunbelieveableunbelieveableunbelieveableunbelieveable!" Roje began to mutter something like, "I wouldn't mind dying so long as I managed to take that human with me…"

Rila cared for her subjects and would undoubtedly be

saddened by Roje's death. I didn't think the dark elf had much of a chance against me, and I trusted that I'd be just fine.

I'd thought that Roje had disappeared somewhere, but then I heard the door creak open, and she entered the room. Clutched in her hands was a chipped and dirtied hand ax.

"Human...how do Her Majesty the demon lord's lips taste... after claiming that her cooking was poison...?"

"R-Roje, stop that."

"Your Majesty, please do not stop me. He has sullied your beautiful lips with his own."

"I-I-I'm the one who always starts it!"

*That's true.*

"Starts what?" Roje stopped in her tracks.

Rila immediately covered her face with her hands.

"I'm the one who's always wanting it. Always, like a beast... What horrible things are you making me say?! A-anyway, stop it."

"It's true," I said with a nostalgic tone. "After you learned about it, you quickly grew insatiable, Rila."

"S-stop talking about that. Stop."

"Your lust was a demon lord in its own right."

"I just told you to stop talking about it! Don't say such things in front of my servant! Think of my reputation!"

Rila began pounding her fists on my chest.

Roje dropped the ax, and it clattered to the floor. She began to back away, palms over her eyes.

"This place is steeped in an aura of happiness! My eyes, *my eyeeeeesssssssss*...!"

It was then that the physician came over.

Apparently, her time collecting herbs in the human lands had helped her develop new medicines. She told us we could stop by anytime.

The physician offered us a digestive medicine of her own making.

"…I must admit, I'm quite relieved nothing serious befell you, Your Majesty. When I came to take you, you expressed great worry about your stomach," Roje said.

"Huh?! Y-yes… That's correct!"

"But…you're a woman now… Oh, Your Majesty…whyyy…?"

Roje dipped to her hands and knees and began to sob. This was the woman who, only moments earlier, was screaming about her eyes. It seemed she was quite the busy person.

Rila and I left Roje to her grief in the physician's room.

"So even you were worried about me, Roland? I see, I see…"

Rila was smiling, grinning, laughing, and making all manner of unusual expressions.

Though the military physician routinely returned to Hell, she seemed to be fundamentally devoted to developing new medicines on the island. She had a Gate set up at the entrance of the barracks and created a path to the place where Delacress the dragonkin had been defeated.

When Rila and I returned home, we made another Gate connected to the island.

"With this, we can get to the military physician anytime. If there's anything wrong, be sure to tell me right away," I said.

Rila had no mana, so she couldn't make the jump herself.

"Thank you. That will help."

I'd ended up taking a day off work without prior notice. I resolved to apologize to Iris later.

"…The diagnosis was entirely different from what I'd expected, you know…," Rila suddenly admitted.

"Hmm? Really?"

Rila fidgeted restlessly. Despite being the one to raise the subject, she didn't seem like she wanted to continue.

"What did you think it was?"

"Th-this is just a supposition…but it's best we talk about it in case it happens in the future…"

I waited for Rila to finish her thought without pushing her.

"…Wh-what would you do…if I was…to conceive?"

"Huh?"

She had taken me by such surprise, I was left dumbstruck.

"A-as I said…was I to become pregnant…what would you think…?"

"If you conceived? If you got pregnant? You mean with my child?"

Rila quickly nodded. She wrapped me up in a close hug and didn't let go.

"…I—I have…no experience…except with you…"

"That's true," I responded.

My thoughts strayed to memories of Milia's family. That was the sort of *normal family* I sought. Naturally, Milia had been born from her mother, and her parents had raised her. Raising children certainly seemed like a *normal part* of life. In which case, if I was to continue pursuing *normalcy*, becoming a parent was a road I eventually needed to travel.

Rila and I had enjoyed a considerable number of sexual congresses, and though I was a bit surprised about the idea, a pregnancy was a matter we'd have to deal with sooner or later.

"I think there's still a disparity between what the world calls *normal* and what I think of as normal, but…when that time comes, I hope that we can aim for *normal* together."

Rila quickly nodded several times again.

Roje had said that when she'd come for Rila, the demon lord had been worried about her stomach. Now it all made sense. Rila had mistaken the fever and fatigue of her stomachache as signs that she was pregnant. Looking at Rila, I began to sense a curious feeling welling up inside me. It was similar to *warmth* but slightly different.

*Maybe I'll ask Milia about it tomorrow.*

"What would you think about a pregnancy, Rila?"

Rila blushed slightly as she mumbled a broken reply. "…When I pondered the idea…I was…happy… Thinking that I might've been with child made me weep for some reason…"

Tears began forming in the corners of Rila's eyes.

I hugged her slender body. Her hair smelled nice. She wrapped her arms around my neck, and we shared a deep kiss.

The Gate outside the house began to glow, and Roje appeared.

It seemed Roje had used the jump.

"Your Majestyyyy. ♪ Where did you go after…leaving me…behind…?"

Immediately, all life drained from the dark elf's eyes.

"You…again… How dare you defile Her Majesty the demon lord's beautiful lips with your own…"

"Funyaaah?!" Rila shrieked like a cat and moved away from me.

"Ah, um, Roje…are you not going back to Hell?"

"I am, but I will be stopping by every once in a while!"

Roje had quickly regained her spark, but Rila seemed very bothered.

"If I may be so audacious, I, Roje Sandsong, would love to partake of your cooking, Your Majesty!"

Roje's eyes were brimming with enthusiasm.

"W-would you?! Do you really mean that, Roje?"

"Of course, Your Majesty…!"

*They certainly have a lovely relationship. I only hope Roje doesn't end up dead.*

"I don't mind if you pop in, but a dark elf would stand out in town even more than a demon," I said.

"A dark elf…? Ha-ha! Ah-ha-ha-ha! I nearly forgot that Roje is supposed to be a dark elf." Rila seemed quite amused.

"What's so funny about that?" I asked.

"Roje, that getup is no good here. Please dispense with it at once," Rila commanded.

"Yes, Your Majesty."

Suddenly, Roje's hair, eyes, and skin all changed colors. I suppose you could say she turned into an alternate version of herself. Her hair became a vibrant green, her eyes were honey colored, and her skin was pure white. She was…

"I see. You're just a normal elf."

"Yes. That is right. Roje is an odd one. Since a normal elf would be looked down upon in the demon lord army, she used mana to disguise herself as a dark elf."

"There you have it. I'll be checking in periodically to see how Her Majesty the demon lord is faring."

"Do what you like," I said.

"Roje, I am no longer the demon lord. Please call me something else."

"Of course. Then, if I may be so forward, I would like to call you Lord Rileyla."

"Mm-hmm. That does not displease me."

With that, Rila and I at last regained our peaceful daily life.

This is a bit of a digression, but Roje tried some of Rila's food and ended up on her deathbed.

I kept an eye on her, but there were a few times when the elf was close to losing consciousness.

"Don't push yourself," I warned.

"Butt out…! This is proof of my devotion…!"

Right after Roje made a big fuss about saying that, she fainted with a peaceful look on her face.

All of that happened after her second bite.

# ◆King Randolf◆

"…Your Majesty, we sincerely thank you for accepting the request of such a small nation."

"Mm-hmm. Seeing as it came from Elvie, Almelia's friend and a hero in her own right, there was no way I could ignore it."

Elvie had sought an audience as an envoy of her home country, the Holy Land of Rubens.

This made the fourth time.

Taking a knee, Elvie respectfully bowed her head before me. Her voice was reserved and respectful. "Once this matter is resolved, let both our countries see this as a great, auspicious occasion."

Elvie was one of the heroes responsible for the demon lord's demise, but she was also a member of the aristocracy in her homeland. Naturally, such a position came with its fair share of responsibilities. During the audience, I spoke to her not as one of my daughter's friends but as Elvie the knight and envoy. It was clear that the young woman felt ill at ease with discussions, however.

...I hadn't told Almelia anything about the matters we were deliberating. Truthfully, I didn't think there was anything I could've said that would've convinced her to attend anyway...

It was fine as long as she didn't rave and shut herself in her room. Not even military force could make that girl do something when she'd made up her mind.

"This friendship between my kingdom and the Holy Land of Rubens will enrich both our nations."

At least, that's what I told myself...

"Yes. I am sure Princess Almelia will take a liking to Lord Fabian."

The letter Elvia had come to deliver was a formal marriage proposal between my daughter Almelia and Prince Fabian of the Holy

Land of Rubens. To put it plainly, it was a political marriage. The date, time, and place for the families to meet had all been noted in the missive.

Oh, how I wished Roland could come with me…

Even if the arranged marriage was a cover for some no-good plot, things would work out so long as he was around.

It seemed unfair to request his assistance in royal matters when he so desperately sought *normalcy*, though.

"How troubling. No… I have decided. There is little other choice. Very well, I will bring Roland with me…!"

Roland had no way of knowing of this decision at the time.

# Afterword

Nice to meet you. I'm Kennoji. For those of you who already know me, I'd like to thank you for buying another one of my books.

This book is the published version of the work first serialized under the same title on the *Shousetsuka ni Narou* website.

In the past, I've written works I knew would be popular, but this time I created a work about something I wanted to write. I quite like cool, callous main characters.

As a result, I really enjoyed myself while working on this. All throughout the process, I was whispering, "You better sell wellllllllll."

Oh, but I always think about things like that when I'm drafting new works. I'm sure I'll say similar things when the next book comes out.

A lot of people helped me get this book published, so I'd like to thank them.

To my editor, who told me what I needed to do, you deepened the work all the more through your precise instructions. What's more, your communication and the incredibly smooth and stress-free production process was a lifesaver. I look forward to working with you again in the future.

To KWKM, who drew the illustrations, thank you for drawing a Roland who was even cooler than the one I'd imagined. I'd also like to thank you for drawing such a cute but no less elegant Rila. I look forward to working with you in the future as well.

Furthermore, to the people in charge of the design and binding, to the salespeople, to the proofreaders, to the employees at the actual bookstores, and to everyone else who was involved in the manufacturing and sales process, thank you very much.

Lastly, I'd like to thank all the readers who bought this book.
I promise this series will only get more fun as it continues, so I hope you look forward to future volumes!

*Kennoji*